THE WORLD, SILENTLY SPINNING

A NOVEL

M.B. MASKOVAS

"The clearest way into the Universe is through a forest wilderness"   —John Muir

"It is horrifying that we have to fight our own government to save the environment"   —Ansel Adams

BOOK CHAPTERS

PROLOGUE

"I'm going to miss my flight," Katy said, trying to keep her voice as flat and emotionless as possible. She resisted the urge to fidget with discomfort on the cold metal chair. To keep herself still, she furiously rubbed the bottom lip of the steel table. She'd been sitting on the very uncomfortable chair in a TSA room at Austin-Bergstrom International Airport for what felt like thirty minutes already. There was no clock in the room. There wasn't much of anything except for her, the metal furniture, and unfriendly Mr. Harris.

"You must understand, ma'am, this is simply standard protocol. All Level 2 and higher scientists are required to submit to searches when flying, even across state lines. You should have been prepared for the security procedures — we won't be responsible for you missing your flight." Mr. Harris of the Science Review Division of TSA dumped her belongings out on the table in front of them as a punctuation mark to his scolding. He had been waiting for her at the end of the screening area when she'd gone to collect her items after getting through security — Katy guessed that, as soon as she'd scanned her ID at the entrance of the airport, they'd known she was there.

He pawed his gloved hands through her belongings, which he had set in between them on the table. Clothes and toiletries were pushed into a rough pile. Katy tried to control her expression as he tossed a handful of her loosely packed underwear onto the growing collection of what she guessed were "safe" or "boring" items. She didn't want to seem embarrassed or afraid — or, worst of all, as if she were hiding something. Her computer and notebooks were put in another pile, closer to Mr. Harris's blue-gloved hands. Those were the items she knew he was going to examine more carefully. After he had fully emptied both of her bags, Katy squirmed with discomfort as he opened her weathered orange field notebook that sat on top. Even though she was careful about what she wrote down, she always worried there would be something they could consider banned material. Scientists didn't answer to publishing committees anymore — they answered to the Science Review Division, which wasn't about science review at all. More like the science silencing committee. Katy cursed herself for not getting to the airport sooner, but her taxi had been late, and she had finished her last shift only hours before she'd needed to leave.

Mr. Harris glanced up at her from the notebook. The look on his face suggested he was trying to scan her for lies like he was scanning her notebook. The notebook only had wing and weight measurements of Mexican Free-tailed Bats. Fascinating stuff. Katy kept staring at him, willing her temper to boil back down. She had just finished a night shift, and it was bedtime. The taxi, the airport, and now Mr. Harris were making it hard to avoid getting mad at something. Mr. Harris was just as good of a target as any. If looks could kill, hers would have spontaneously lit his perfectly pressed suit alight. It had been a while since she'd had a run-in with the SRD. Every time, she felt violated and afraid. In fact, she had avoided this entire situation in May by renting a car and driving from Berkeley, where she was a Ph.D. student, all the way to her appointed Summer job in Austin, Texas. Unfortunately, on the way back, she didn't have twenty-six hours to burn. She needed to get back to prep for the start of the semester.

"You're not going to find anything interesting in there. Just my notes from my Summer job." The clock was ticking if she wanted to get onto her flight — or, she guessed it was, from this timeless room of inquiry. She shuffled her scuffed leather biker boots under the table, unsure if her toes were tingling from anxiety or from the uncomfortable chair.

He didn't look up. "What was your Summer job in Austin?"

"I have been performing a census of the local bat populations. I responded to calls about dead bats, collected them, and evaluated their cause of death." Katy watched the typical response — a nose wrinkle of disgust.

Mr. Harris looked back down at her notes, clearly satisfied with her response. He flipped through the pages, looking for anything that would incriminate her, and then tossed the notebook aside and began examining her other papers and documents. He was rough with her things, and Katy wondered if it was on purpose — a show of force. Her eyes wandered to a pair of crumpled blue underwear that had been tossed very close to the edge of the table.

"Have you been researching any prohibited subjects?"

"No." Katy made eye contact, hoping her dark eyes could tell his way-too-blue ones to screw off, and then looked away to stare at a dust bunny in the corner of the windowless room. She watched as the air conditioning moved it back and forth, waiting for his next question.

"Have you taught any prohibited materials, or do you intend to teach any prohibited materials at the public university?"

"No."

Mr. Harris's pen scratched away at the small white notepad he was holding. He set it aside and pulled out one of her full-sized notebooks and shoved it in front of Katy. She could see one of her recent projects, with a scratching of calculations and some other sketches.

"Can you please state the type of calculation you have written here?" He kept his eyes locked on her.

Katy nibbled the inside of her lip, swirling her tongue around the back-end of the lip-piercing stud. She did that when she was trying to stall for a moment to think.

"Mr. Harris, would you like a lesson in population modeling?" Katy had let the jest slip before realizing what she had done. The tickle of humor left her with a feeling of dread in her stomach and tingling toes.

"A real answer, please, or I will have to destroy this information as prohibited material and report it to the SRD as a violation." His lips were drawn into a tight line, and Katy couldn't help but notice a tiny bit of toothpaste at the corner of them.

"It's a new type of model for estimating a population of group-species based on human factors like city expansion. It's not finished yet — just an idea." Katy tugged more on the lip stud with her teeth. She hoped that answer would satisfy him.

Mr. Harris stared at her for a long pause, his eyes breaking contact with her to look back down at the document. Then, he looked back up.

"Well, you aren't being very compliant, but we have documented everything here. You will be hearing from us if you are breaking any laws."

Katy heard, *Stay in your lane, scientist*, in both the tone of his voice and the way he looked at her books with disdain.

She swore being a scientist would be entirely illegal soon. The world wasn't far off from that point, anyway. The SRD was in charge of keeping scientists from investigating any topic that was considered "propaganda and lies." *Don't publish anything that will contradict the President's current ruling on global warming or any other topic. Don't rile up the masses about natural disasters. Don't point out that the ongoing loss of biodiversity will cause a failure of crops and bankrupt the world. Don't talk about new novel coronaviruses coming out of China and how they could spread across the United States.* Katy had become a scientist to make the world a better place, but even as she'd started college, America had already been in a state of rapid change. The advances they had made in the last decades were being wiped away by a conservative government who'd finally managed an authoritarian control over its citizens.

Mr. Harris threw the last document back onto the pile. There was a knock at the door then, and he turned to open it, exchanging some words with a person Katy couldn't quite see through the cracked door. She leaned forward to try to listen, her ribcage digging into the table. When Harris turned back to her, she quickly moved back in her chair.

"You're free to go, ma'am. Please gather your belongings and exit to the right. You'll need to run to catch your flight — they're already boarding." He opened the door wider and stood at the entrance.

Katy scrambled to her feet and began shoving her clothes back into her suitcase by the handful. She hoped they would all fit now that they were no longer neatly rolled.

Outside of the room, she took a moment to breath in the air of freedom and listen to the busy and urgent sounds every airport makes. The loudspeaker echoing, the constant hum of rolling suitcases and travelers talking loudly on their cell phones. Mr. Harris had kept following her every move with his eyes, as though the way she packed up her items would reveal some secret she was hiding.

With her moment of peace over, she began sprinting through the airport. Her heavy boots pounding on the high-traffic carpet, she dodged an elderly couple in matching gray sweaters, and a mom struggling with her three crying children as she tried to get them to step onto the moving walkway. Katy glanced up and down from her ticket to the gate numbers as she raced by.

"C32, C32, come on. B50, ugh," she mumbled to herself as she tried to pick up the pace.

She arrived at the gate huffing for breath as the last few passengers scanned their boarding passes. The gate attendant smiled and scanned her ticket and wished her a pleasant flight. Katy grunted in response. Barely even 8 a.m. and today was already turning out to be a long-ass day.

A few minutes later, she settled into her window seat and then watched as the ground shrank below her. Her ears popped and the plane fell into a relative silence, which she was grateful for. She leaned her head against the vibrating windowpane and dozed for the short flight.

GOING UP

She kicked a cigarette that had been spinning endlessly at the bottom of the escalator as she climbed out of the train station. Then, she had a feeling a sudden wetness on her upper lip. A heavy drip of something fell down her lips, chin, and onto the stairs in front of her. She looked down and saw a sizable spatter of blood on the grooved steps of the escalator.

"Oh!" She clasped her hands over her bleeding nose and fished in her pocket for a slightly used tissue she'd put there earlier that morning. Clasping it over her nose, she felt wet-warmth through the tissue almost immediately. The escalator ended and the bright morning sun hit her face and made her squint as she stepped off. Katy almost never got bloody noses; she couldn't even remember the last time she'd had a bad one like this.

She tugged the strap of her worn green backpack farther over her shoulder with her free hand and hunched over to the bus stop, hoping that the tissue would last her until she found another one in her pack. A handful of her waist-length raven black hair was sticking out at an odd angle at her shoulder, pinched in the backpack strap. It waved and bounced as she stalked toward the bus line headed toward Berkeley.

A dusty public bus pulled up to the curb, filling the air with the smell of fuel. *Right on time.* The doors popped open and Katy, in her own world, went to climb up the stairs before seeing anyone getting off. Her hand was still clamped to her nose, and she was fishing in her backpack side pocket to see if she had one more tissue. When the man coming down the stairs ran right into her, she barely even knew what was happening before she started falling backward down the steep stairs of the bus. Her arms wind milled, hitting the side railing but not quite grasping it. The concrete sidewalk met the back of her head with a stunning blow.

Instead of what she expected to happen next, which was for her to have a concerned person ask her if she was okay, something entirely different began to happen in the still-stunned moments after she fell. The large man with a beer belly who had run into her raced over her prone body and onto the sidewalk, and a flow of other panicked people followed. Katy curled up into a tight protective ball against their kicking and stepping feet. She squeezed her eyes shut and focused on surviving this moment — whatever it was. Rough hands grabbed around her armpits and hauled her out of the panicked masses.

"Hey, hey! Are you okay?" A man was looking at her with wild, wide eyes. Down his scruffy beard were streaks of crimson.

Katy was shaking and still dazed, her eyes zoning in on his public-transit badge. The bus driver. She was able to nod numbly. *Yes, I think I'm okay.*

He guided her over to the bus shelter and sat her down.

"Stay here. I'll be back to check on you." With that, he ran back to the crowd gathered on the sidewalk in front of the bus.

She rubbed the bump on the back of her head and brought her fingers to her face. There was some blood there, but when she went to feel the bump again, it felt like a small-enough cut. She was lucky she hadn't cracked her skull open. Already, her head was aching. She looked down at her shirt, which was spattered with blood from her nosebleed.

Once she had settled her own nerves, she watched with morbid interest and curiosity as the scene unfolded in front of her. She could feel her heart speeding up at the sight of so much blood. It seemed as though every passenger on the bus had gotten a spontaneous nosebleed, like her, and all at the same time. An older man was crying, holding out his hands covered in blood as two other passengers ushered him off of the bus. As Katy watched, her curiosity began to turn back into fear. It was horrible. A woman was cradling a young baby in her arms, and Katy caught a glimpse of the child's tiny pink face as it screamed. Blood was running from the child's tiny nostrils, and her mother was trying to control her own nosebleed. The sight made Katy feel slightly sick to her stomach.

The passengers milled around the bus stop, one woman offering her pack of tissues to the other bus-goers. A few older children wailed as their parents hushed them and tried to wipe their bleeding noses. The sight of the kids in such a panic worried Katy. The middle-aged woman who had been handing out tissues began to gather people and check on them, delegating tasks and soothing babies. Soon, the raw panic of the passengers began to calm slightly, though the scene had attracted the attention of everyone else at the regional station.

Katy kept her place at the bus shelter — and considered dialing for an ambulance. She put away her phone only when she heard the middle-aged woman who'd taken the lead of the situation calling. Anyway, Katy was the one who'd fallen and bumped her head. Someone else should do it.

"I can't get through!" The woman hung up after some time spent standing away from the crowd with her phone to her ear. Her face was paper white.

Eventually, the woman tried again and got through, at which point she told the operator that everything seemed fine now, but that a disease control professional should come and file a report. The group slowly began to disperse. Taxis pulled up and families climbed in while others walked off to the BART station. The bus driver began unloading remaining luggage from below the bus. Once he was finished, he walked back over to where Katy was sitting.

"Are you okay, ma'am? I was very afraid for you there." He looked down at her with concerned crinkled eyes.

"Yeah, I'm okay. Just a bit freaked out." Katy felt a familiar feeling — fear of exposure. Was there another pandemic on its way? Her skin crawled at the thought, and she shivered. The reason her grandparents weren't alive anymore was Covid-19. She didn't want to think about what would happen if another pandemic swept through the country.

"Well, the busses are all canceled for now. Can you find a ride home?" he asked.

Katy nodded, and the driver headed back to his bus. There was no way she wanted to get on a bus right now anyway. She got out her phone and tapped on "Danielle" in her favorites.

Danielle picked up after two rings. "Hey, Katy, sweetie, are you back in town?"

"Yeah, I am. I'm at the train station. Actually, I had a bit of a fall and all the busses are canceled. Would you maybe be able to pick me up?"

"What?! Are you okay? Should we go to the emergency room? I can't imagine braving Cali traffic for anyone else. Drop a pin and I'll be there in, say, thirty minutes or so? I don't know what the traffic will be like."

"Thanks, Danielle. But, no, I don't think I need to go to the emergency room." Despite the situation, Katy smiled at Danielle's concern as they said their goodbyes on the phone.

She made herself as comfortable as was possible on a hard metal bus-stop bench. Today was a day of uncomfortable metal benches, she mused to herself.

After wiping off her face as best she could, she opened up the bag she'd had tucked between her knees and took out one of her tattered journals. The last stretch of traveling was always the hardest, when you knew you were almost home but not quite. She'd hoped to make the connection between the airport train and the bus and be on her way already. Instead, she opened the notebook to a drawing she'd started last week — one of a Mexican Free-tailed Bat. During her Summer research job in Austin, she'd picked up a special bat a few days before she'd been set to leave. The bat had had odd speckles of color in its dark gray coat; a variation, a potential new trait. When she had lifted it from the hot road, it had still been alive, and it had bared its teeth at her as she'd cupped it in her heavy work gloves to get a closer look. Tiny, bristling, and full of glimmering white teeth. The young bat had probably hit a window or a car while flying with its group early in the night, and now been regaining its strength. She'd let the bat glare at her and dig his tiny claws into her gloves as she'd examined him for injuries. Such beautiful little creatures, she was proud to help them. After a few minutes of resting in her hands, the bat had seemed more alert, his ears flickering this way and that in listening to the night. With a pump of her hands, she had let the bat fly into the air, back to his everyday life.

Her mind was lost in that moment as she darkened the lines of the sketch and added some scribbles of observations to her notes. She was jolted out of her memory as someone sat down next to her. It had been long enough since the bus incident that new visitors to the station had started to filter in, not seeming to notice the lightly blood-spattered sidewalk.

She gave the woman a polite smile and went back to her sketch, running her thumb over the deep indent in the paper left by her pen.

"You're an awful nice artist, hun," she was interrupted.

"Thanks," Katy said, smiling politely and going back to the sketch.

"You could try to draw something nicer maybe. Bats are so nasty."

Katy opened her mouth to object. To tell the woman that they were misunderstood creatures, that they were beautiful and kept bug populations low and had the cutest fuzzy little faces. Instead, she shrugged slightly, keeping her universe of batty secrets to herself, and squeezed her nails into her palm as she made a fist.

"Where are you from?"

The voice just would not leave her alone. The woman had tilted her body more toward her, feet pointed toward Katy. Conversation time.

"Portland." She was always amazed that people would keep going when they were given so little. Her pen sat idle in her hand at this point as she alternated between staring at the empty bus in front of them and down at her notebook, trying to shrug the woman off.

"No, I mean where are you *from*," the woman said.

"I said, Portland. I lived there until I moved here six years ago." She wasn't going to give in to that repetitive question.

The woman opened her mouth and closed it again, and finally gave up on the discussion.

In the tense silence, Katy closed her notebook from prying eyes and watched the cars whiz by on the highway, waiting for a familiar one to pull into the station and save her from this place. Finally, the worn-out Toyota Corolla she'd been expecting rolled up where the busses were supposed to park. Her friend stuck her head out the window and tilted down her oversized sunglasses.

"Beep beep, all aboard the Danielle bus!" she yelled toward the bus shelter.

Katy was already laughing and walking toward her.

"Shhh, Danielle, you're not supposed to stop there!" She tossed her bags in the back and got in the passenger seat, reaching across the center console to give her best friend a big hug.

"I missed you, girl! Now, let me see this bump on your head. Ewwww, blood is so gross!"

With Katy's coaching, Danielle cleaned the small gash on the back of her head. Danielle also found some makeup wipes in her car, which Katy used to wipe off any remnants of blood from her face.

"Oh, totally weird, but I had a bloody nose earlier, too. Wouldn't that be a weird new disease? Instead of the flu, we all get bloody noses?" Danielle chattered in the car.

Katy knew Danielle talked like this when she was nervous. After a few minutes had passed and they'd gotten onto the highway, they fell into a worried silence as they both contemplated the events of the day.

Katy's eyes drifted closed as she leaned against window.

GILLS

The world came ringing back to her with a cymbal crash, and she was standing on the sidewalk in front of her home. She didn't remember being dropped off by Danielle in front of her apartment. The last thing she remembered was falling asleep as the car rumbled down the highway. She didn't even remember saying goodbye to Danielle.

Maybe her head injury was worse than she'd thought, and she should have gone to the hospital.

She looked around, bewildered. All seemed normal with the world; it was just her that felt off. A foul smell met her nose and she wrinkled it, looking down. On the sidewalk in front of her was a dead squirrel. It had been there for a while, its intestines pulled out. The damage looked like it had been done by a cat, and the tangle of pink intestine strings appeared sticky in the morning air. The smell was as all dead things smell. Sickeningly sweet, a stomach-churning *wrong* smell. The dead squirrel's tongue was lolled out in a macabre scene, eyes starting to shrivel into little prunes in the sockets.

"Poor thing," Katy murmured and felt wetness on her upper lip.

She reached up and wiped with the back of her hand, seeing that it came back red. She pinched her nose and walked to her front door while struggling with her bags, reaching into her backpack pocket with her free hand and searching for the keys. The bloody nose had come back. She told herself it was the dry airplane air, trying not to think about all the people at the bus stop with the same problem — panicking and tripping over each other as they'd run off of the bus. Almost crushing her in their fear to get out. *Airplane air, airplane air.* She almost muttered it under her breath as she fumbled with the keys to the apartment.

She opened up the door and tossed her bag in the small entryway. Kicking off her shoes, she stepped into the bathroom and peered in the mirror. The blood from her nose had started to dribble onto her lips and chin by the time she'd noticed. Taking fist-fulls of toilet paper, she held it to her nose and stared at her reflection. She ran another clump of toilet paper under the water and used it to dab the blood off of her lip piercing and chin. She then patted the bags under her eyes and ran her free hand through her dark hair. The silver hair around her temples shimmered in the fluorescent bathroom light. The hairs were almost becoming full chunks of gray now on the sides, in a stark difference to the rest of her raven black hair. Now in her late twenties, she'd started to see the first grays when she'd been barely in her teens. The doctor's chalked it up to genetics, though she didn't know her biological family to confirm that theory.

She puzzled at how she could have missed the last half of her drive with Danielle and saying their goodbyes.

Maybe working night shifts for so long and the lack of sleep over the last few days just caught up to her. The human body was never meant to be nocturnal, and it sure took a toll. Yeah, lack of sleep was making her mind wonky. Though, she couldn't think of a time in her life where she had ever spaced out like that. People always told her she was too sharp for her own good.

Trying to shake off the fog of the morning, she walked into her bedroom/kitchen. The studio apartment was small, but she didn't mind. A little den for a small person who liked her privacy. The apartment had plain off-white walls, with a kitchen that was open to the quaint living room where a single worn-out velvet sofa faced the TV. Her low-to-the-ground bed almost bumped shoulders with the TV console. Now, she set her laptop on the kitchen counter and opened it, then starting the hot water for some tea. She had the feeling of fine-grit sand behind her eyelids, with a raw and tired feeling, and her head had a deep pressure at the back; a throbbing headache was beginning to form. Honestly, she felt terrible. Bad enough that it could be a bad cold or a flu coming on. She had also taken small wads of toilet paper and jammed them up both nostrils to stop the bleeding, adding to her misery. The kettle started to make ticking noises in the background as it heated up — a friendly sound to break the stale silence. Katy looked through her Facebook feed, eyes half open. But they went wide as she scrolled through the posts, and her stomach knotted up.

Alex Mathers: Had the craziest nosebleed this morning. I don't normally post things like this but man it was nasty

    Comments: OMG me too. Maybe this is the new Coronavirus. This is the end!

Another Ph.D. candidate from college had posted a selfie of her holding a tissue to her face. A news article followed: *Unexplained Nosebleeds Across the Country Leaves Experts Stunned…CDC is evaluating preliminary results but has yet to comment further.*

    Katy read through the first part of the article. Some public spaces had been shut down due to mass nosebleeds, and pathologists were already looking for some kind of virus that could be behind it. The part that really made Katy's stomach roll came when she read, "The incidents aren't isolated to the United States. Countries all over the world have confirmed that they have seen the same phenomenon, all around the same time today."

    Katy slammed her laptop shut. Nope, she couldn't handle any more of that today. She wondered if maybe she should see the doctor about her head-bump, and then the fear of infection overpowered her again. The kettle screamed for attention, so she flicked the stove off and soon went to settle down on the couch with her tea. She hugged the mug to her chest and leaned into the couch cushions, staring at the blank TV. She tried to pretend that she was safe where she sat, and that whatever was happening outside would pass her by if she stayed inside long enough.

But the mint tea tasted stale. It had been sitting in the cupboard since she'd left at the beginning of the Summer. She frowned and took another sip — a bit too much. The tea burned the tip of her tongue. She looked to the windowsill to see if her plants were still alive as she pressed her burned tongue against her teeth. Seeing them, she made a mental note to thank her neighbor Tim for keeping them alive and to ask for the spare keys back. He'd enthusiastically taken on the task, but she suspected it wasn't because he had a love for green things, though she was happy for the help. Despite having lived here for several years, she didn't know many people. Her work colleagues all lived on the other side of town.

The ceiling rumbled above her as the neighbors upstairs moved around, and she could almost hear their conversation. She strained to make out individual words and drank her tea after it had cooled some. Kicking her feet up on the coffee table, she wiggled her toes, leaning back into the couch cushions. Her eyes wandered from place to place as she let her mind relax and settle — the dust lining the TV stand, the crease where the wall met the ceiling and the painter had missed a spot…. She relished the quiet of home.

Her mind wandered to her position at the UC Berkeley, a job that she would need to go back to tomorrow. The pressure on the state-funded schools to conform to the new teaching curriculum meant that many of the science disciplines were being thinned. Graduate students and professors who refused to accept the new anti-climate change propaganda were being forced from their positions. It was a mystery why she'd managed to stay around. Probably because she had chosen the most incompetent advisor, who was actually a geologist instead of a biologist — or, at least, that was her guess. Nobody cared about geology unless it had to do with oil and gas drilling. Government officials would regularly scan through the scientific articles ready for publication, forcing some into silence, or worse. Only rumors, she knew, but some of her colleagues had dropped off the map in a very suspicious manner. The school always had some excuse as to what had happened. *"Professor Richards took a unique opportunity at a foreign university and decided to move his whole family for the position."* Yeah, right.

So far, Katy had managed to avoid having her research snuffed out by never publishing, and by obscuring her true research and interests. Her specialty was the human impact on ecosystems, both world-wide and smaller intricate systems. She was the mathematician of humanity's destruction. Her calculations were damning. She specialized in the information the current government wanted to call blasphemy. With the number of professors who had been forced out or quit, though, Katy was teaching several lectures by herself and still on a graduate student's pay. The content she was asked to teach was neutered at best and lies at worst. Katy hated every lecture she taught and cringed every time she had to tell a lie to maintain the new curriculum. The only thing that stopped her from teaching older, more correct material was that government moles would attend lectures to keep the faculty in line.

It was horrifying to see how quickly these changes happened. Only a few years ago, it had seemed like the world was finally starting to acknowledge the damage humans were causing, and universities had been teaching a new generation how they could innovate and reduce humanity's impact on the world.

She felt a sense of hopelessness as she tugged at the string of her teabag and let the steam soothe her aching sinuses. Maybe she should consider a new line of work before she starved to death or was thrown in jail. It made her blood boil that studying the way the world worked could be something punishable. How had they stooped so low? She remembered the way that the security agent had treated her at the airport, and finally the encounter caught up to her. She felt a few angry tears well up in her eyes.

She was tired and felt like shit, and the headache that had started earlier was really gnawing away at the base of her skull.

After having herself a little cry, she wiped her cheeks and stomped into the kitchen. She yanked on the handle of the fridge. It set a yellowish glow on the kitchen, and as she'd expected, it was empty. Except for one Tupperware shoved to the back of the middle shelf. She had been gone for the whole Summer, though, so whatever had been in there must be absolutely horrible. Despite knowing that whatever was under the white lid was no good, she peeled the top up. Sludge and fluffy black and green mold greeted her, bristling at being disturbed. She held her breath and looked again. Small orange speckles of mold also covered one edge of the container. That was beyond saving. She imagined what it would be like to scrape that alien beast into the trash and rinse out the container, and the smell that it would create when met with the hot water. Nope. The container went into the trash, despite the guilty feeling she got about throwing away plastic that would end up in a landfill. Her stomach rumbled and she sighed, and she considered ignoring the feeling and climbing back onto the couch. If she melted into the plush cushions and watched movies all day, she might be able to distract herself from her current worries. Instead, she checked the freezer and was equally disappointed when she remembered that she had cleaned it out before leaving.

Despite her plans to become one with the faded upholstery of her second-hand sofa, she packed her reusable grocery bags and changed into a fresh white T-shirt and worn-out boyfriend jeans with holes in the knees. Comfortable, practical, and best of all, free from the "post-travel" grime. She threw her ruined shirt from earlier into the sink. She knew it was probably too late to scrub out the bloody nose stains, but she'd try later. She wiggled her feet into her well-worn combat boots and stomped out the front door.

Twenty minutes later, she was in the grocery store. The lights hummed, and she stood in front of the produce section with a heavy basket in the crook of her arm. The tinny sound of fake thunder made its weak crack over the speakers nestled above the produce—the grocery store's coy way of warning customers that they were going to mist the vegetables. She plucked a package of peppers from the display and stepped away before the hiss of the sprinklers came on. As she continued to browse, a store worker looked up at her from where he was listlessly re-organizing a mountain of potatoes. He didn't smile... just stared at her for a second and then looked back down at his root vegetables. *He looks how I feel*, Katy thought to herself as she tried to brainstorm what food she would need for the next few days. She hadn't brought a list or planned any of her meals yet. The artificial glow of the store made it hard for her to think, too, and her body was telling her that it was time to go to sleep. Her night shifts for three months that Summer hadn't been long enough for her to truly become nocturnal, but it had sure been long enough to make it painful to switch back to normal days.

After what felt like an eternity of indecision over which brand of chicken to buy, she stood in the checkout line. The flimsy plastic handle of the grocery basket bit into the crook of her arm as she waited, and the headache that had plagued her all day still creaked away in the back of her skull. Everyone else in the store seemed low energy, just like her. The woman behind her with her crying baby was half-heartedly soothing him as he wailed in the cart. Her eyes were hollow with dark circles around them, and she stared ahead as she tried to stroke her child's angry red head. The child got even more red in the face and balled up his tiny fists.

The cashier didn't even look up as he swiped Katy's goods across the scanner, tossing them to the end of the conveyor. Katy thought she saw a crust of blood lining his nostril. She shivered again, trying to push irrational thoughts out of her mind. What if there was a terrible new strain of the flu going around? Another coronavirus here to force all of the world to stop and hide inside? Or what if the pollution from manufacturing and burning fossil fuels was finally getting to be too much for human bodies to bear? *What if, what if, what if.*

As she drove home, she rubbed her temples at every stoplight. When she made it, she sighed with relief as the door swung shut behind her and she kicked off her shoes, letting them tumble where they wanted. She could hear the upstairs neighbors stomping around still. The dog next door barked its tired old bark, sounding like gears grating on and on. The vet had done a horrible attempt to cut its vocal cords—a procedure of debatable humanity, where a veterinarian removed a dog's ability to bark at full volume. *If you can't give a dog enough love and attention that it feels the need to bark all day at nothing, then you probably shouldn't have a dog.* Since the surgery, the dog sounded more and more like an old wheezing man yelling into the night, "HEY, HEY, HEY!" Katy never complained like some of the other neighbors did. She felt bad for that old dog. His owners didn't give him what he needed and then punished him for calling into the night, "Hey, I'm so lonely, I need something, ANYTHING." And no one ever answered, so he continued on barking.

In the city, even when it's quiet, it isn't quiet. There's always the slight hum of traffic, the small ticks of engines and clocks, and the slams of doors. The jungle sounds of a city, the sirens that are the howls of the city-wolves and the rumbles of neighbors moving their furniture… they're the real thunderstorms of apartment living. She listened to the jungle thrum and shout as she unpacked her groceries. It was easy to find space in the empty fridge. She left out ingredients to make some pan-fried veggies and eggs, one of her go-to easy meals. Pulling a mushroom out of the package, rustling the plastic bag, she examined the earthy thing with its bottom full of wet gills. Touching this intimate part of the plant, she ached for the feral wetness of the forest near where she'd grown up. The way that moisture hangs from every tree and fern to create a blanket of wildness. The quiet that is so powerful it flaps wings against your eardrums as they ring from the absence of motor and people sounds.

She began slicing and tossing pieces into the heated butter in the pan, listening to the hearty sizzle. There was a knock at the door. After a brief wipe of her hands on her jeans, she walked to the door, standing on her tiptoes to see out the peephole. Tim was standing there with his telltale curly black hair falling into his eyes. The latch clicked as she unlocked the door and opened it.

"Hey." She kept the door partially closed and peered out of it like her home was a secret she needed to keep. Which she immediately felt foolish for since he had been spending time in her apartment for several months now, caring for her plants.

"A woman of few words, as always. What's up, homie, how was your Summer?"

"Fine." She kept the door cracked, feeling a growing hostility even though she knew she should be grateful for his house-sitting. Her head hurt, and her thoughts hadn't stopped racing since that morning. She just wanted this day to be over so she could fall into bed and hopefully sleep through the night. Talking with Tim wasn't getting her closer to bedtime, and when she felt like this, she found that her mouth got ahead of her and she would end up saying things she should have kept to herself. Katy did have a bit of a temper, she knew. It was always boiling under the surface. Most of the time, she kept it under lock and key and covered it with a stony silence plenty of people knew her for.

"Do you mind if I come in for a minute?" He tried to peer over her into the apartment.

Katy shrugged and opened the door wider. He gave her a big goofy smile and came in.

"Damn, what you cookin'? It smells hella good in here." He walked into the kitchen, and she slowly followed. She hated how he bobbed his head like a chicken when he talked, but assumed that he thought it made him look cool. She resisted letting her eyes flicker into an eye roll.

"I was just making some food... was there something you needed?" She gave the mushrooms on the stove a cursory stir. Turning her back to him, she added some spices as he wandered into the living room.

"So, where's your boyfriend?" He was looking at the big piece of art taking up the majority of the living room wall, a gift from her best friend. It was an angry painting of black and red in smudges and swirls of smoke. Danielle said it reminded her of Katy. Plus, no one else at the gallery had wanted to buy it off the artist; it was too creepy. The piece of art looked out of place in the bare apartment with only college student-level furnishings, but she loved it. She would never get tired of staring at that painting, getting lost in every splatter of paint and dark smear.

"I don't have one." She kept her back turned to him, not wanting to see his reaction. Tim was nice enough, but he was dumb as a stump and talked like a sixteen-year-old. She knew he'd been fishing for that answer. He'd hinted at his interest in her on several occasions.

"So, that means you're single, then?"

Her shoulders knit together. The same repeated song and dance. Over and over again. It was like certain conversations with people were automated, and you had no choice but to repeat a dialogue. Once again, she felt herself growing hostile, although she knew he didn't mean any harm. What was it with her today? The headache, bloody noses, and lack of sleep were really putting her in a weird mood.

"No," she said simply and turned around after pulling the pan off the burner. "Thanks for watching my apartment while I was gone, but I really need some space right now." Her cheeks were burning red and her chest felt tight. Maybe it was the long day of travel, but she felt like she might cry if he kept looking at her like he was.

He appeared shocked, and she could see a series of emotions cross his face. Confusion, disappointment, for a moment indignant rage that someone could reject him like that, and then his expression shifted to that of a kicked puppy.

"Yeah, sorry, I just wanted to drop off your spare keys. I didn't mean to bother you." He pulled the keys out of his pocket and put them on the table. "I'll be seein' ya, Katy, enjoy your dinner. Peace out."

He closed the door carefully behind him. Katy let out a long sigh of relief and locked it. Conversation ended. She looked back to her phone, which had been sitting face-down on the table, and she let her deep breaths guide her stampeding heartbeat down to a normal speed. Breathe in, three counts. Breathe out, three counts. Her nostrils flared as she tried to suck more air into her lungs, willing it to calm her down and bring sense to her irrational behavior. Her hands felt cold and wet as she wiped them on her jeans. Why had being in that situation scared her so much?

She felt guilty for the way she'd treated Tim and made a note to apologize when she got the chance… or worked up the nerve. The Summer, with minimal interactions with other people, had left her rusty.

A few minutes later, with her lazy dinner prepared, she sat down at the dining room table and scooped up mouthful after mouthful with mechanical speed. Not really tasting much, just eating. Her mind began to wander to the nosebleeds again, and she got a morbid feeling in her stomach. She'd always had an overactive imagination— one that got her into trouble when there was nothing at all happening in the outside world to threaten her.

Before she could start thinking about the downfall of humanity, Katy unlocked her phone.

The call picked up after only two rings. "Hey, Mom."

"Hi, sweety, I was wondering how you were doing. Did you get home okay?"

The familiar voice tamed her worries for a moment. "Yeah, it was fine; my flight was on time," she lied. She wanted to hear about ordinary things right now. Getting interrogated about doing math and working at the university wasn't normal. And being knocked over at the bus stop and getting trampled wasn't normal. The whole world getting bloody noses definitely wasn't normal.

"Your dad is out at the range, but he was hoping you would call today. I'll tell him to call you back tomorrow. Everything here is fine. There was a big ol' racoon in the yard last night—it set off the motion lights and woke us up. He didn't manage to get into the garbage, though."

Her mom continued telling her how the weather was in Portland, what projects her dad was working on around the house, and more details of their daily lives that she was no longer a part of. Katy smiled and laughed at her stories and told her about how she'd found the cutest baby bat on one of her last days on the job. And, most of all, Katy told her how happy she was to be home, and that she couldn't wait until her next trip to Portland to visit. They began planning a Spring camping trip where they would meet in the middle between Oregon and California and then postponed their planning when Katy's mom realized how exhausted Katy was.

Katy passed the rest of the day by keeping moving. It had only been around 3 p.m. when Tim had come by, though to her it had felt like three in the morning. Her head still hurt, but she managed to calm down with some food in her. She was determined to get back to a normal sleeping schedule as fast as possible. About 8 p.m., she gave in and dove into her bed. She fell asleep almost instantly.

LET IT BLEED

Katy woke up the next morning as light tickled her face from the window where she forgot to close the blinds. She rolled out of her bed, pulling her hair out of the ponytail she kept it in while sleeping. Her hair swished free, silky and straight as it brushed the top of her waist. Sitting up on the edge of the bed, she moaned and tried to blink through the sticky feeling around her eyes. Her full night of sleep hadn't felt satisfying, and she swore she felt exactly the same as she had the day before. The good mood she had fallen asleep with was long gone. Tongue heavy and dry in her mouth, waking up when she should be going to sleep felt awful. *Never again*, she thought. *Never again will I work a night shift.* Katy knew this was probably a lie she was telling herself. She loved working with nocturnal animals, and she was pretty sure that the city of Austin would ask her back next year.

As she leaned over to pull on her pants from the day before, she felt a heavy wet drip from her nose and looked at the wood floor between her bare toes. Her nose had started to bleed again. She cupped her hand to her face, craning her neck forward to avoid getting blood on her shirt. Scrambling to the bathroom, she almost overturned the coffee table on her way.

The flow from her nose was thick and heavy, and there was a high ache in her sinuses and across her temples—a hangover without the enjoyment of a night before.

"Ugh, what the hell is happening?" she asked herself, looking in the mirror and prodding at her lymph nodes. Her neck didn't feel swollen at all, and her throat wasn't sore.

"Huh!" Katy spun at a noise near the entryway. For a moment, she thought she saw something dark crawling across the floor. Her heart raced and she felt her skin flush. But a second look proved there was nothing there but the morning sun showing through the front window. It must have been the shadow of a passing car through the frosted glass.

"Why am I so damn jumpy?" She could feel blood seeping through the tissue she had clutched to her nose and pulled another one out of the box on the countertop.

Katy wiped up the blood on the hardwood floor in the other room before retreating back to the bathroom. She decided the only possible way to shake this hangover feeling was to take a long, hot shower. When she stepped in, the steaming water sent a wave of soothing goosebumps over her skin. She sighed, swaying her body in the stream. Almost immediately, the ache in her temples faded away. She let go of her nose and let the blood drip down her lips, chin, and neck. Looking down, she watched the blood mix with the water branch down her breasts and stomach. She felt a telltale cramp low in her stomach and saw a similarly branching trickle of blood down her inner thigh. It spiraled down her knee, wrapping around her calf before disappearing in the flow of water at her feet. Good. Might as well bleed everywhere when it's time to bleed. She washed her hair and felt rather satisfied and free, bleeding in the shower. She stood in the hot stream longer than she needed to, eyes closed. Lost in the moment and surrounded only by the sound of rushing water.

Her nosebleed had ended by the time she was ready to get out. She blew her nose into her hands one last time and let the gobs of red, sticky snot rinse from her palms in the stream before turning off the water. She fluffed a towel up and wrapped it around her shoulders and reminded herself to check the news again to see if there were more reports about the bloody noses. Maybe the CDC had made a statement by now.

A few minutes later when she was finished drying off, she scrolled through the news on her phone as she packed up a bag to head to the lab. She wanted some time to organize things before the semester started, and to get through some paperwork. The news only had similar stories to those she'd seen yesterday—no new developments. No one knew what was wrong, but more people were having bloody noses.

An hour later, the lab was empty when she arrived. The hallways of Berkeley were so quiet before the semester started. Only a few people strolling the campus; even the vagrants who were infamous around the area weren't around much. Her lab sat in the basement of the earth sciences building, with humming old yellow lights that made everything feel more tired and isolated than the lab actually was. She walked into the office, which was attached to a quiet lab with rows of black tables wiped clean. A few jars lined the walls, and an illustration of the anatomy of a fruit fly hung on the far wall. Tucked into the office were two worn-out desks with chips in the cheap varnish. The one to the right was hers, and everything was where she had left it. Stacks of expensive college textbooks, the lamp that sometimes needed a good smack to turn on, and even her chipped mug with a stain from tea. She guessed none of her lab-mates had come back from the Summer break yet. After wiping off a layer of dust, she began organizing her files and getting settled back into her work.

"Heyyyyyy, Kitty Kat Kat Kat!" a voice echoed through the empty lab.

"Hey, JD." She straightened her back from the hunched position she'd taken up in front of her computer.

"Looook what I haave!" JD was holding a lab rabbit. Its tiny white nose wiggled back and forth, big white ears glued to its body. He walked over to her and held out the rabbit.

"You know you're not supposed to love on the lab animals," Katy said as she accepted the rabbit from the massive man and cradled it in her arms. Rabbits were so soft. It always amazed her how something could be so cloud-soft. Why did nature make something that spent most of its life trying not to get eaten so damn soft?

"Whatever you say, math lady. You act all mean, but you're really a big ol' softie, aren't ya?" JD was a pillow of a man, with a scruffy light-brown beard and wide shoulders, wide chest... well, wide *everything*. He was one of the few other Ph.D. students left in biology. A lot of his work was sponsored by pharmaceutical companies that required animal testing. He hated hurting the animals and would secretly take some of the rabbits home or take them outside to play when no one was looking. He was a good guy. Katy liked him, despite the fact that he was overly affectionate and disrupted her work. She couldn't say no to holding a soft rabbit every once in a while, though. She imagined that JD was a big rabbit himself— all soft fur and no bite. Last year, she'd finally asked him why on Earth he was working in such a position when it made him so miserable. He'd told her that he used the money from his research, which was abnormally high for a research position, to pay for his mom's medical bills. Such a sad story. He'd wanted to be a veterinarian but had ended up here instead.

"How was your Summer?" She looked at the strawberry red eyes of the bunny as she spoke. They always just looked like stuffed animals... no expression in those marble eyes. It was hard to tell if the animal actually enjoyed being held, but she sensed no tension in the powerful hind legs that could be tightly wired for a big jump at any moment.

"Oh, it was pretty quiet. I worked on projects here most of the time. It's so quiet here during the Summer, though, I missed having you around!" He paused. "Not that you make it much louder." He giggled at his own joke.

Katy just narrowed her eyes at him. Then the corners of her mouth tugged in a subtle smile.

"You were doing that bat thing in Austin, right? Doing a census of the population for the city?" He somehow produced another rabbit from behind him—a laboratory magician.

"Yep. It was alright," she said. She kept petting the rabbit she held. Moving up to the long, delicate ears, gently pulling one and then the other in her hands. The rabbit didn't seem to mind. It was a stuffed animal that pooped, after all.

"That seems like such the perfect job for you to do. You're, like, a vampire or something. No, vampires are too scary. I just think you'd like it cause it's spooky." He smiled wider.

"Bats aren't spooky, JD. They're just misunderstood. They're actually just as cute and fluffy as this rabbit... except they sometimes have rabies." She made a mock snarling face, and JD shuddered.

"Well, bat lady, I've got to take these little fluffers back to the animal lab before anyone else comes in and catches us. I'm glad you're back!" He tucked the rabbit he had been holding under his arm like a football.

Katy sighed; the warmth of the bunny in her arms was soothing. Still, she handed the rabbit back and turned toward her desk again.

"See ya, JD."

She pulled out her notebooks from the Summer trip and added them to the pile on the corner of her desk, trying not to think about how roughly they'd been handled at the airport. She sat in silence, bunny-free, and updated her files with notes from her Summer work. She let herself get pulled into the flow. File this, note down that. Stare at one of her formulas for a while and let her mind wander off on a tangent. Every once in a while, a new idea for a model to test out would come to her and she would scribble a new line in her to-do list.

Her attention snapped back to the world around her and to the clock on the wall. It was already two in the afternoon. Something was wrong. Her ears buzzed into tune with the world around her, similar to the way she'd felt when she'd gotten out of Danielle's car yesterday. A bit confused, jarred. As though someone had smashed a cymbal right above her head, letting the metal rings deafen her before the symphony started.

There was screaming outside her lab. She stood up so fast that the chair toppled to the ground behind her with a weak crash.

"JD?" she tried to call over the screaming, walking as quickly as she could down the hall toward the animal labs.

Her heart was hammering in her chest and her breath had caught in her throat. No one was in the hallway—it was just her running toward that unearthly scream. She recognized the scream as she got closer. It was a rabbit death scream. Rabbits were quiet creatures, and one of the only times they made sound was when they were completely terrified. The shriek that resulted was ear-piercing and desperate. That sound was coming from down the hall… but not from one rabbit, like sometimes pierced the night when one would be scooped up by a fox or an owl. It was all of them. All two hundred rabbits in the test labs. As Katy got closer, she could also hear the desperate squeaking of rats adding to the symphony of screams. The racket was so loud, it hurt her ears terribly as she quickened her pace down the yellow-lit hallway. She gulped a stone down her throat as she flung open the heavy double doors to the lab where JD worked.

"JD?" she yelled over the deafening sounds.

Every cage in the lab was bristling with an animal either clawing to get out or screaming its head off. She clapped her hands over her ringing ears as she took in the scene in front of her. Paws thrashed at the mesh and bars, teeth gnawing at every possible way to escape. Rabbits jumped desperately at the solid walls of their cages, almost bashing their own heads in. She could see one rat killing another one in its fear. The lab was laid out with one long wall of cages, the one she was looking at now in horror. The rest of the room was two or three times the size of Katy's lab, with surgical steel tables lined with equipment. On the far end from the screaming animals was JD's small desk with his run-down computer.

Willing herself to get closer, she peered into a rabbit's cage. It shied away from her in terror and kept screaming, mouth open wide. Two sets of yellowed buck teeth served as punctuation marks in its open, raw red mouth. Blood was trickling from its small nose, down into its gaping mouth. The red was covering its top buck teeth, and she didn't dare reach in and try to comfort the thing. Turning around, she looked for JD again. At his desk, there was a cup of coffee still steaming. As she leaned over the desk to check for signs of JD, she spotted something. On top of a page titled "Pain responses in various species" were three drops of bright red blood, seeping into the paper and making it warp. She spun around, heart stampeding through her chest. Breath was difficult as she took little sips of air. The fear in the room was almost a tangible thing, pressing down on all of them.

There was a loud *BANG* from behind her. Her first thought was that her eardrums had burst, and Katy cried out and pressed her hands harder to her ears as she dove onto to the ground on pure instinct. The screaming stopped then, and flecks of something landed on Katy. Something wet and warm. Her heart still tried to claw its way out of her chest, like the rats in their cages. She slowly raised her hand up and touched whatever had hit her. Her fingers met something hot and wet.

Her hand trembling, she looked to see what it was…. chunks of flesh, with soft fluffy white fur. She turned, stiff and slow, and saw that, two cages up from the rabbit she had been looking at before, there was a mess in the cage. There was no more rabbit—only pieces of it. An ear that was stuck to the roof of the cage plopped down into the middle of the cage, soaking in the red wine mess.

Katy climbed to her shaky feet and felt wetness on her back. She twisted to see the back of her T-shirt. It was also covered in clumps of rabbit gore. She held her elbows out in an awkward square, not wanting to touch anything. All of the other rabbits seemed okay, despite their previous screaming. Except that every single one of them was staring at her. Every rat in the lower cages was also up on its hind feet, peering at her from their smaller containers. Katy shuddered in horror, turning away from their gazes. Their silent stares were too much after the screams.

Katy stumbled out of the room and into the hallway. Her terror turned to anger as she stood there soaking in hot dead rabbit. She could feel stinging tears forming in her eyes, but she forced them back.

"JD, WHERE THE FUCK ARE YOU?!?" she screamed, her voice cracking a bit. She whipped down the hall, slamming open every door to every other lab and room. She finally reached the men's restroom and barged in.

"JD, you better be in this fucking toilet taking the biggest shit of your life with headphones on, or I'm going to kill you."

JD turned and looked at her from the sink, where he was holding wads of toilet paper to his face. The sink was a splattered mess of blood. His eyes widened as he looked at her, and she could see his bottom lip dropping below the fluff of toilet paper in his nose to gape at her.

"What. The. FUCK. Is happening?" She pointed down to her shirt, where every fleck of rabbit stew was widening into splotches as it was absorbed into her clothes. Her nostrils flared as she stood there staring him down.

"Whoa... is that blood?" JD couldn't stop staring at her while squeezing the bridge of his nose.

"Yes, it's fucking blood, JD. Also, do you have ears? Because they should be fucking bleeding right now, too, after hearing what just happened in your lab. I'm sure the whole campus could hear it!" She turned to face the mirror, gripping the counter with both her hands white. Her arms were shaking, and even though she was looking at her reflection, her wide eyes weren't seeing. Her mind raced, trying to rationalize what she'd just seen in any way possible. The gap between her knowledge of what was possible and what had just happened was gnawing away at her. That rabbit's blind red stare and red-stained teeth flashed in her mind. All of those rabbits looking at her... she felt like they were probably still staring at the door she'd fled through. Her shoulders knit together as she trembled. And then she realized that she didn't have a bloody nose like JD did. She didn't know what that meant, but her panic was setting in.

JD reached out a hand, about to place it on her back to soothe her. An inch away from her terrified, angry back, he pulled away again.

"I don't know, Katy." He made a hiccupping crying noise and then went on, "I started to hear something in the lab, but I was already here dripping like a faucet. Then the world started to spin, and my head felt like a big ol' balloon. All of a sudden, it was over, and I heard you slamming every door on the way here." He hiccupped again. His eyes were welling up with tears that splashed down his cheeks.

Katy sighed, making a ticking noise with her mouth. She turned to JD and put her hand on his upper arm. Focusing on his fear and upset was much easier than trying to handle her own. Feeling his slightly clammy arm under her own sweaty palm helped steer her heartbeat back into a normal direction, and she looked up at his ghost-white face. Her anger and fear had sent him over the edge. His lip was trembling, and big fat tears had begun rolling down his round cheeks and into his beard. The tears were big enough that one even splashed all the way onto his T-shirt, leaving a dark mark.

"I know, JD. Don't cry. It's okay."

The last thing she'd said was a lie. It definitely wasn't okay. There was rabbit puree all over her; apparently, rabbits were exploding, and no one could stop bleeding from their face. Something was happening. Something big. She could feel a crawling, terrifying pain in her belly.

He cried anyway. Meanwhile, she got as cleaned up as she could, using the foaming soap in the bathroom to scrub her face and hands.

She pulled her T-shirt over her head. Katy felt vulnerable for a moment, but JD didn't even take a second glance as she began scrubbing the shirt in the sink. She turned the water as hot as it would go and pumped handfuls of the foaming soap into her palm before scratching at every stain. After wringing it out, she pulled the still wet and blood-stained shirt over her head again. It stuck to her body, and she could feel the water cooling against her skin, making her shiver, but that was better than the alternative.

JD's nose finally stopped bleeding, and he very gingerly removed pieces of rabbit that he noticed in Katy's hair. Chunks of rabbit had landed in her hair and on the back of her neck. He did so so carefully that she could barely feel it when he found a piece, as though she was an animal with its foot in a trap, and he knew if he tugged wrong, she would bite.

When Katy showed JD the rabbit cage, he cried again. His eyes were bright and puffy at this point, and there was dried tear salt starting to collect in his beard. Katy helped him scrape some of the remains into specimen jars so that they could analyze it later.

"We need to wash the cage now, JD," she said, pulling out the cleaning supplies from the bottom cabinet. "We can't leave it like this or it will start to stink."

He looked green.

She sighed. "Okay, how about you go get me a Coke from the vending machine upstairs? I'll get started." She tossed him quarters from the pocket of her worn jeans.

Blood and gore never bothered her that much; she could take a distanced view of the bits and clean them without feeling sick. If the dead bats didn't bother her, neither would an exploded rabbit.

What *did* bother her was the other rabbits and rats in the room. Some of them had gone back to regular rodent activities, burrowing in their corners or drinking from their water bottles. Others still stared at her with their beady eyes, unmoving except for their wriggling noses and twitching whiskers. She tried her best not to look up from what she was doing, but she could still feel their bright eyes on her as she gathered up the cleaning solutions and rags to start scraping up their friend from the floor.

JD floated out of the room, in a daze and surprisingly light on his massive feet. Katy started to scrub. The industrial cleaning solution stung her eyes and nose, but she desperately wanted the evidence of whatever had happened gone. She scrubbed so hard that a trickle of sweat formed down her brow. JD was gone for a long time, and when he finally came back, she was already done with the cage, with a pile of bloody rags in the trash and one shining, empty rabbit crate in front of her.

"Sorry, Kats." He slumped his shoulders a bit and handed her a soda without looking at her. It wasn't exactly cold anymore.

She popped the tab and examined her colleague. He still had a smear of blood in his mustache. He smelled like cigarettes, and she realized he must have bummed one off of a passing student outside. She understood. She didn't smoke, either, but she also ached for something to dull her grinding nerves.

"Did you drive here?" she asked.

JD nodded. He had been staring into the empty cage as she'd sipped the sugary drink. She realized that she had skipped lunch going through her research but wasn't a bit hungry until the sugar hit her belly. The carbonation skipped across her tongue that was still burned from her tea the day before.

"Want to drive me home?" she asked. It wasn't a request. He nodded and pulled his thick keychain out of his pocket. She hoped he was okay to drive. She didn't know how to drive a stick.

"Rabbits are already fed and taken care of for the day." It was one of the first things he had said in a while. His voice had that croak of someone who had been crying their eyes out.

The sun was getting low as they walked across the parking lot to JD's old Ford truck. The sunset glow didn't feel as beautiful as it usually did. Katy knew it was her imagination, but to her, it felt like the world was dying. The last rays of light gave everything an unnatural glow as she pulled herself up into the tattered passenger seat. She shivered despite the moderate temperature, rubbing her arms as she looked out across the parking lot.

HEADLIGHTS

The rest of the herd was about a mile away; he could smell them on the crisp Autumn night air. His wet black nose flaring, taking in every scent. Testing the air for danger. The young buck wove through the pine trees, picking his way carefully. Winding his hooves into the best places to step so he wouldn't make too much sound. He must get to the herd. Even in the woods, he felt exposed. A predator could find him at any moment, and without the other deer, he would be the only target. His wide ears swiveled and twitched at all of the sounds, velvet-covered antlers dipping as he stepped. He was a tawny brown and white shadow passing through the trees, trying his best to camouflage with the oak scrub brush and the rough-barked pine trees.

Leaves crunched under his weight as he picked up speed. He must get to the herd.

The grazing was better at lower elevations, but it was dangerous there. At dusk, they would pick their way down, down, down to the open fields to eat the cool and dewy green grass. Perfect, delicious, and out in the open. He could almost smell the grass from where he was, along with the flowers and weeds that would help him grow strong for Winter. His wide liquid-black eyes tried to take in as much of the forest as he could as he steadily traveled downhill. Without a Summer of grazing on the fattening grass in the lower valleys, he wouldn't survive the scarce Winter, when his only food would be the dying grass and the roots buried beneath the snow.

The way began to flatten out, and he was faced with the first opening in the trees. He could see the next grouping of trees across from a wide meadow, lit by the bright moon above. Beautiful… and dangerous. Maybe on another day he would stop and graze in such a place with the herd, but today he was alone. His muscles tensed and coiled as he stood at the threshold. Then, with a mighty spring, he bounded across the meadow, leaping high in the air and tucking his nimble legs to his body. Moments later, he was safe in the trees again, his heart pounding.

A noise to his left made him spring into the air one more time, so that he almost collided with a wide pine tree that had been split in two by lightning. He turned to the source of the noise and saw a fox staring, face in its permanent grin as it stalked mice in the long grass. The fox turned and trotted along on its way, leaving the buck to catch his breath under the wide-needled branches of the pine tree.

As he walked away, a tuft of his coarse tan and white fur caught on the rough bark of the tree and stayed there, a waving flag in the light breeze of the evening. The next morning, a squirrel would take it into his den to use as bedding.

Giving back.

The herd was very close now; he could smell his mother and other familiar deer. Their closeness filled his heart with hope as he picked his way along the ever-sparser trees. Soon, he would be grazing with them and flicking his ears back and forth in pleasure as his herd-mates did the same, in silent agreement that they had found a good place to graze.

The terrain grew steep again, and he had to lean back as he picked his way down the rocks and trees. In front of him was a wide-black expanse, just wide enough that he thought he could not jump the whole thing in one go. He knew this hard ground—his mother had shown him when he'd still been a speckled fawn that it was safe to walk across. Yet he did not trust it, especially when he was so close to being reunited with his herd. So, he tensed his powerful muscles again, winding up his hindquarters against the steep hill and then letting them unwind in an explosive motion, launching him across the road.

The light was so bright and fast-moving, rushing toward him as he flashed through the air, elegant form lit by the spotlight. The car rushed forward, barely beginning to break. The tires squealed, and with his ears pinned back to his head, he could only continue his flight through the air.

The driver of the car squeezed her eyes shut as the passenger screamed. "Deer!"

Then, silence.

He stood on the edge of the road, staring at the steel monster that was watching him with bright wide eyes. The people in the car remained just as still, slowing their hammering hearts as they looked at the green-flashing eyes of the buck who stood safely on the other side of the road.

Once he'd gathered his wits about him again, he turned his tail to the car and disappeared back into the brush. Relieved. He crossed the road and was safe. He would never stray from the herd again. He trotted through the scrubby bushes and low trees, toward the groomed expanse of green that awaited him. From here, he could make out the white-tailed rumps of his herd-mates.

He was so absorbed with his destination that he failed to notice the mountain lion, coiled up on the rocks above him. She was waiting patiently in silence, as she had been for hours. Tucked against the shale and rocks, invisible but to the sharpest eye.

The buck did not have the sharpest eyes, and he was trotting out in the open, still too far from the herd.

The teeth and claws came, slicing open his back and neck like a hot knife. The mountain lion lashed and bit as he bucked desperately with all of his strength, attempting to remove the heavy hunter from his back. The mountain lion's claws scrabbled for purchase on his skin, ripping open more wounds that stung in the cool air. He cried out, and the heads of the herd rose from their sweet grass. She clung to his back as he bucked and whipped his neck, biting and clawing and snarling as she did so. He used every ounce of his strength to kick and buck the monster from his back. The pain boiled as blood streamed from his wounds. His muscles burned, and he could feel his strength fading—her hold was too strong.

The ground rose up to meet him as he crashed into the dirt, the mountain lion on top of him; the feline's puncturing front teeth sank deep into his neck. Crimson bubbled around the mountain lion's tawny jaws, soaking both of their fur, sticky and hot. The two made eye contact as the last life ebbed out of him, with his wild liquid-black eyes locking with the golden ones of his conqueror. He moaned one more time, looking at the green fields that he'd come so close to.

He would never leave the herd again.

OMISSION

The truck rumbled to a stop, pulling up behind Katy's parked Subaru. JD turned off the engine and sat there looking forlorn.

Katy cleared her throat. "Um, do you want to come in?"

The last two days had been so weird. The idea of being alone, which she normally liked, was too much right now. She wanted some company. During the drive, she had considered trying to get Danielle to come up from the city to spend the night with her, but JD was here already, and she found that she actually quite liked JD.

"Okay." He waited for her to get out of the car before he climbed out and followed.

"I'll make us some tea or coffee. Which do you want?" She unlocked the door and opened it wide. As she turned back to usher him inside, she saw Tim standing on the sidewalk across the street, staring. She made brief eye contact before she closed the door, her cheeks flushed. *It's not what it looks like*, she told herself in silent explanation.

JD walked into her small apartment, looking around the cramped entryway while kicking off his shoes. He looked like a giant climbing into a hobbit hole. Any other day, Katy would have had a small chuckle about it. Today, Katy hurried into the kitchen. She didn't want to watch him as he examined her home. It was only one room; he didn't need a tour. A steaming mug of mint tea was calling to her, to soothe her rumbling stomach. She didn't feel ready for food yet, even though it had been that morning when last she'd eaten. No, every time she thought of food, she got a bad feeling and heard rabbits screaming. JD stood silently in the living room, looking around without really seeming to see anything.

A few minutes later, they took their drinks to the back porch. The porch looked out onto the empty yard where the semi-mute dog lived. They watched the dog root around in the patchy grass after he'd spent some time looking up and wagging his tail at Katy and JD.

They sat in silence. Cupping their mugs to their chests. As they did, Katy looked up at the almost cloudless sky. She saw a flock of geese in the dying light of the early evening... but they were flying North instead of South. Winter was coming, and they were almost home, but they were flying in the wrong direction. She shivered even though it was a warm day, in the 60s still. The old dog looked up and started baying endlessly at the geese. He barked as though they were the last things he would ever get to bark at. His bushy tail stuck straight out behind him, quivering with every grating bark.

"Do you ever get the feeling that something isn't quite right in our world?" JD's voice interrupted Katy's stare at the awful old dog. She grunted in reply. "Like, how did we end up like this? Slowly dying while this country falls apart," he continued, hugging his mug tighter to his chest.

She was surprised at the melancholic tone coming from someone she'd always imagined as endlessly positive. Her eyebrows rose up in surprise as she examined him. He was slumped, his eyes glazed over in thought. She thought she could see a bloodstain on his flannel.

"I dunno, JD." She took a premature sip of tea, her nerves raging in response as she burned her tongue—again.

"We know this earth is dying because of us," he went on. "Science proves it, not that it even needs to at this point. The signs are there. We know it, and what have we done? Increased oil and gas production; shut down the solar industry that was taking off. It's illegal to drive electric cars, Katy. *Illegal.*"

"Mmhmm, I know. I used to have one." She rolled her tongue back and forth on the roof of her mouth. She'd replaced the electric car with her parents' old Subaru. Not that she needed the all-wheel drive in California most of the time, but it was a reliable car that she could camp in if she ever wanted to.

"People can't even live in some parts of Florida, and forget about Louisiana 'cause of the water levels." He started gesturing wildly as he spoke. "The hurricanes have gotten worse and worse. The fires have devastated some parts of Cali. People haven't even tried to move back. Like, why do we live here? It feels so hopeless," he added.

The fires had gotten closer to the bigger cities recently. There was a lot less forest to burn now, but every year, it seemed like all of the forested states became giant tinderboxes. Katy was painfully aware of this, and every time news of a new fire came, her heart broke at the beautiful ecosystems being decimated.

Now, though, Katy just nodded. She was listening, but her mind had gone to other places. She was thinking about keystone species—species in a certain ecosystem that didn't appear to be particularly important at first glance, but in actuality held together the whole mechanism. Wolves in Yellowstone Park had been the example they'd given in her undergraduate classes. Over and over again, they would talk about the Yellowstone wolves. In 1995, scientists had gotten approval to let a small number of wolves that had used to be native to Yellowstone back into the park area (much to the raging disapproval of farmers and landowners nearby). Then, something unexpected had happened. The whole park had started functioning better. The wolves kept the elk population down, and with the elk population down, trees and foliage grew better. With that, the beavers (another much-hated animal of farmers) began to reshape the waterways in the park again.

Yellowstone had bloomed back to its former glory, all because of the wolves. Now, under the new Administration, the ban on killing the wolves had been lifted. Reports now suggested that only a few wolves were left in Yellowstone again, all of them with a price on their head. The elk population had already begun to grow.

Every subtraction humanity made had effects that couldn't even be predicted, offering a cascading mess of destruction. So, perhaps JD was right... it was all going to shit.

JD stopped talking—a full pause with his head tilted toward Katy. She realized he wanted her to respond.

"I don't know, JD. All I know is, this is a shit time to be a scientist." Her tea was finally cool enough to drink. She took a sip to punctuate the end of her statement.

"Yeah. No offense, but I don't know how they haven't stopped your research yet, Kats. I mean, I'm getting paid the big bucks to torture rabbits 'cause the pharmaceutical companies still need someone to torture rabbits for them. All you do is talk about how humans are ruining the earth and pick up dead things." He chortled at his own joke. The laugh still sounded half-hearted compared to his vampire jab earlier that day.

"Someone's got to pick up the dead things."

"And this is why some people say you creep them out."

Katy knew that JD wasn't creeped out by her, even if he didn't share her calm regard for death. He stared at the ground in front of him. "JD?" She nudged him.

"Oh! Sorry. I guess I'm still feeling a little cloudy from earlier." His coffee was now cold, she guessed. He swirled the glass a bit, took a sip, then shuddered.

"Sorry," she said, assuming she'd gotten her proportions off. "I don't normally drink coffee." She shrugged.

"It just messes with your adenosine levels."

"Yeah, I still like the taste of it." He tried another sip. "Except maybe when you make it."

Katy laughed. JD smiled wide, and she felt her mind settle for the first time since the incident.

"Actually, I don't know how much longer I'm going to be a scientist, JD," Katy admitted, drooping with thinking about her encounter at the airport.

JD set down his much and tilted his head at her.

Katy sighed. She had said too much already, and now she would have to share her feelings. "At the airport, I was detained. They looked through my research and my computer and everything. They let me go, but I don't think it's the end of it. I was scared in that room, JD. I didn't know what they would do to me."

JD's hand covered her own, and Katy startled. The warmth of his skin on hers radiated up her arm, and she felt her cheeks flush.

"I think if I keep going, something bad might happen to me. Maybe I should just quit now while I'm ahead and find something else to do." Katy looked down at her knees, kicking her legs back and forth where they dangled off the edge of the porch. What would she do, though?

"I think you should fight back, Katy. What you're doing matters. What we're doing matters, and someday people will look back on history and we'll be the heroes."

Katy laughed. "Such an optimist, JD. I'm not going to make any decisions today. Especially with all of this crazy shit going on."

"Yeah." He was quiet again as they were both unpleasantly reminded of the rabbits in the lab. They didn't need to say anything more on the matter. Both of them had the memory like a dark cloud over them, and it wasn't time yet to talk about the weather.

The sun dipped below the horizon, leaving a warm orange glow in the sky. The silence was long but comfortable between them as they watched the sunset. The neighbors came out with a plastic bowl for the dog, all but tossing it onto their back patio. They didn't even give a second glance to Katy and JD.

"Would you maybe... want to stay the night?" Katy blushed, wondering why on Earth she was asking. "I'll sleep on the couch—you can take my bed since you're taller and all. I just still feel weird about everything and it's pretty late. I know you live far away." She felt like her cheeks were going to light on fire.

"Yeah. Honestly, I was dreading driving home. If it doesn't put you out too much, I'll take you up on that." JD smiled.

Beside him, Katy squirmed. Would she even be able to sleep with another person only a few feet away from her? The idea of being alone and thinking about those rabbits, though, all staring at her, was much worse.

After they took their mugs inside, they ordered pizza and spent the evening watching TV and talking. They talked about everything except the nosebleeds and the exploding rabbits. It felt good to have a normal conversation. It felt good to be with JD.

Sometime later, once she had finished brushing her teeth and getting ready for bed, Katy settled onto the couch, trying not to be painfully aware of the other person only a few feet away from her lying in her own bed. She could hear him rustling around, probably also uncomfortable. The night was another noisy one, with the people upstairs shuffling around and cars going by outside. That gum-toothed dog was yelling again, "HEY, HEY, HEY!" at nothing in the backyard. She fussed with her hair a bit, piling it on top of her head and then burrowing down into the pillows.

It felt like hours that she lay there staring at the popcorn ceiling, chewing on the inside of her lip. Finally, JD stopped moving around and her eyes grew heavy.

She startled awake, the way you do after a falling dream. Something was wrong. All of her limbs flailed out, grasping for the solid feeling of the bed. Except that she was on the couch. Her hand hit the coffee table, hard. She grunted in dismay after re-orienting, and then it hit her. What was wrong. It was so quiet, her eardrums throbbed from it. Her wide-armed flailing and subsequent collision with the coffee table were the only noises she'd heard since awakening. No dog, no cars going by. She couldn't even hear JD moving or breathing. She squinted in the low blue light. The quiet was still pressing down on her. Not the roaring silence of a forest found after going far off of a well-trodden path, but the silence of a field before a hawk swooped down. It sounded like everything was hiding, waiting for something terrible to hunt them.

Soon, the sound of her own heartbeat was pounding in her ears, and she feared that the hawk waiting in the trees would hear it. She thought she could feel wetness on her upper lip. She wiped at it with the back of her hand.

"JD?" she called out. Her voice felt weird, hoarse from sleep. It traveled through the silent-trembling air and fell short.

"JD... are you there?" She swung her legs underneath her, but the lump on the bed still didn't move. Her ears felt like they were on fire, and her forehead was throbbing like something with sharp claws was trying to scrape its way out. She couldn't remember ever having a headache this bad. She stumbled, groaning at the pain and pressing her palm to her forehead.

She flipped on the lamp. The light seemed like it came on slowly, chasing out the tendrils of the dark. *Not normal.* She squinted in the brightness as her eyes adjusted. The fluff of JD's hair was still on the pillow. For a moment, she felt guilty for calling out to him—he was probably sleeping. The feeling wouldn't go away, though, and the pain in her ears and head was calling to her, *something is wrong. Something is coming. Something is coming NOW.*

She clapped her hands to her ears and screamed.

The scream was instinctual. Katy didn't think she had ever screamed like this in her whole life, but it was ripping out of her now. It felt like her head was going to explode like a watermelon dropped from a fifth floor.

The pressure was building behind her eyes and nose, and her ears felt like red hot coals on the sides of her face. JD sat upright in the bed, eyes not seeing, and he also began to scream. He screamed like the rabbits had been screaming in their stainless steel cages that morning. A piercing death scream. The kind of sound one dreaded hearing when walking alone in the forest, and right now, Katy was alone in the forest. He screamed and screamed. With a force of will stronger than almost any other in her life, Katy stopped herself from making the horrid sound. She managed to stop screaming. Her head was swimming with the pain and her eyes were watering from it.

"STOP, STOP, STOP. JD, STOP!" Her hands clapped to her burning ears, and she felt wetness on her palms.

Broken from her terrified stupor, she rushed to JD, slamming her shin into the coffee table as she did. She climbed across the bed toward him, fighting the agonizing pain in her head. She straddled JD's hips, grabbing his shoulders and squeezing.

"JD, I'm here, it's okay. JD, STOP!" she tried to tell him. Her voice was drowned out by his screaming. He kept looking past her shoulder.

"JD! Stop, you're scaring me!" She shook him a bit. All that happened was that a trickle of blood, which had already been welling in his nostril, dripped down his mustache and into his mouth. Then, that noise, the screaming, wasn't coming from only JD. She heard it coming from every apartment and home nearby. A terrible big band of screams, like a rolling emergency siren lighting up the entire neighborhood. Every person, sitting upright in bed to scream while their throat clawed at them to stop. The roar was like hundreds of planes all flying overhead, close to landing, all at once. Or a million waves crashing on the same shore, or the drone of cicadas, but much more sinister.

Katy let go of JD's shoulders to hug her ears again. He might be screaming, but she was the frightened rabbit. Frozen with her ears pinned back to her body, knowing that the hawk was already there with claws outstretched. Something else was in the room with them, ready to pluck them from the bed.

JD focused, his eyes finally meeting hers. He didn't stop his blood-curdling scream. At this point, she figured he should have run out of air, but the scream went on. He looked so scared, his eyes pleading. His arms went up to wrap around her shoulders—a full, reassuring touch, even though he didn't seem to have control over his vocal cords. She pulled herself into the hug, letting go of her ears once more. The damage to her eardrums was done, and everything sounded cloudy.

But JD's warm solid body beneath her began to feel not so solid. JD's hands gave her one last squeeze then and went slack. His skin rolled and bubbled. She closed her eyes, thinking back to the rabbit that morning.

It ended with the loudest bang she had ever heard. She fell into the now wet space where JD had been.

The world went black.

NEGATIVE SPACE

She opened her eyes to see sunlight streaming through the blinds. For a few moments, she lay there in the sleepy calm of the first few moments of being awake. The moments where you haven't quite remembered the world around you or your worries from the previous day.

And then, last night stabbed her in the chest. She became acutely aware of a damp feeling down the front of her body. Her heart thundered. Slowly, very slowly, she craned her stiff neck down and pushed herself up in the bed. Below her was a still-wet and mushy blood-stain. It didn't seem big enough for all of the blood and organs inside of a man the size of JD. Instead, the puddle looked small enough for Katy to curl up and fit inside of its runny edges. No explosion all over the room, but no JD, either.

Was last night a dream? Touching her now crusted-over ears, she decided it was not. She stood up, legs wobbly. Her head was mostly clear, but her hearing was nothing but a blanketed fog, like there were pillows clamped over the sides of her head. She pushed herself off of the bed. The world swam as she stood up and almost went black again. Her splitting headache from the night before kept a slight hold on the peaks of her temples. Swaying on her feet, she managed to find her footing and take a deep breath in. Nausea made her mouth water and the pit in her stomach flip and roll.

She walked around the apartment, peeking into the bathroom with some last hope that JD was taking a shower instead of having been reduced to a puddle of red on her white sheets. After that, she drank a glass of water and sat perched on the dining room table, picking at the scaling dried blood that was matted into her hair and crusting over her ears. Finally, she picked up her cell phone and dialed the foreign-feeling numbers: 911.

She turned the volume of the phone up as loud as it could go and pressed it to her ear. The pressure made her ear and headache. It rang and rang and rang. She hung up after a minute of letting it ring and stared at her phone. She redialed and tried again. *No answer. No answer to 911? What kind of sick trick is that?* She tried the police department line next, and then the local hospital. Answering machines.

"What the fuck?" she asked, her voice sounding far away and muffled in her own head. She paced back and forth from the dining table to the cool tiles of the kitchen.

She called JD's phone, and it vibrated next to her bed. She let her phone drop away from her painful ear and watched his iPhone dance around on the nightstand. She finally hit *END* when it was about to dance off of the table.

"He just went to get us coffee. I just had a REALLY bad dream, and I have my period," she told herself, looking down at her pajama pants. They were covered in blood. "Yep, bad period."

Nothing to do but wait for him to get back and tease him about leaving his phone behind. She turned on the TV. Pre-recorded stations and a documentary about hoarders. She picked up and unlocked her phone again and checked Facebook. It seemed as though no one had posted in the last six hours or so.

She unlocked and opened the door to the back porch. It was a little bit too cold to be sitting outside in her tank top and flannel pajama shorts, but she curled up on the chair anyway. The thought of changing clothes hadn't hit her yet. She just kept puzzling over what had happened to her. And she listened with her damaged ears. The blood on her pants was starting to shift from crimson red to a rusty brown. A deep bone-rattling shiver kept her company through the ache of her head and the buzz of her ears, but the cool air helped soothe the pain in her temples as everything crumbled around her.

No cars. No neighbors making noise. And no lawnmowers going, from what she could hear as she strained to understand the world through her burst eardrums. Katy figured that was what had happened, at least—she had burst her eardrums. She knew people could still hear a bit if that happened, but she wondered if she would have permanent hearing loss. Her ears just hadn't been able to handle the pressure of whatever had happened. The pain she'd felt last night had been partially relieved when the pressure in her ears had released. Now, they hurt, but her head still hurt more.

The wind kept whispering through the trees at the end of the street, though she watched it more than heard it as the trees gently waved, and she watched as a bird flitted from a rooftop to the yard. She thought she saw something move in the neighbor's bare yard. Yes, there, something was stirring under their deck. She jumped off the deck and hopped over the low fence. Her feet cried on the rough ground, but the sensation was just a tiny prick compared to the rest of the pains in her body.

"Hello?" she called out.

No one responded, but she saw a pair of brown eyes shining at her from under the deck, and then a wet nose. The neighbor's dog poked his head out. He was a mangy lab-mix, a tawny color with black around his muzzle and a white diamond on his chest.

"Hey, buddy." She crouched down, turning her body slightly away in a non-threatening gesture and reaching out her hand. "Hey there, whatcha doing down there?"

The dog army-crawled more of its body from underneath the deck.

"Yeah, there you go, it's okay, sweet thing," she said, beckoning with her hand. The dog crawled closer. His whole body was shaking, and his tail was glued between his legs. It felt like hours before his wet nose bonked into the skin of her hand.

She didn't pet him, though—not yet. After a minute, she got up and went back inside, leaving the chain-link gate between the two backyards open. He followed her up onto her deck, but waited at the back door, staring at her carefully. His tail was sweeping low behind him.

There was no way she could go into work with a headache like this and the thought of red stains on her mattress. Maybe she was having a mental breakdown. If she was going mad, she wanted to do it in the privacy of her apartment and not in a lab.

This is what you get when you try to bury your problems. They will come crawling back up, evolved. It wasn't how she might have expected going mad would feel like. She could still recall her everyday life, and she felt... well, normal, except for all of the aches and pains in her body. She wondered what it would be like to be in a mental ward. Would they let her visit the woods? Go on hikes? Or would she always sit in flimsy pajamas, staring at the white walls like she'd seen characters do in the movies?

"This is how I would go," she said to herself, massaging the sides of her head. Pushing on the tender muscles made them scream for her to stop, but the pain made her feel more in control.

"What a strange way to go mad." She stared at the bed where JD had been just the night before.

A wave of nausea hit her as she stared at that red spot. Doubling over, she vomited on the floor at the foot of her bed. With her hands planted on the ground, she panted, spitting out the last string of spit that attached her to the mess on the ground in one long rope. Her mouth watered terribly. She stared at a clean spot of the hardwood, willing the nausea away.

DIGITAL HUM

Beeeep. Through her muffled world, she could hear the answering machine's greeting.

"Mom? Dad? Mommy… something bad happened. Why won't you call me?" Her voice wavered as she rocked back and forth, curled up on the dining room chair.

Shivering, she set down the phone and walked out the front door, still barefoot. JD's truck remained parked out front. Katy opened her mouth to scream for help, but the fear inside her made her wilt instead. She went back inside and tried calling more people. Her head hurt too much to drive. The headache was almost blinding at times.

And even when the pain had subsided, she was too afraid it would come back while she was driving to try taking her Subaru out. Why wouldn't someone just call her back?

She waited two and a half days in the silence, in a daze. She stared out the window and called 911 every hour. The phone would sit slack in her sweaty palm while she waited between tries. The bloodstain on the mattress started to smell and get hard around the edges. Barely eating, barely drinking, she slept at random periods when she wasn't staring out the windows, looking for some sign of life.

Still, she didn't hear a single car outside—no neighbors coming and going. The silence and her damaged eardrums left a dull ringing hum that was persistent and maddening. The food in the fridge started to run out, and she realized that she'd been sitting in the same blood-soaked pajamas, hair unbrushed. Her menstrual cycle was in free flow, adding to the chaos. She did nothing to stop it. Her thighs were sticky with her own blood, her pajamas ruined. Most of the blood around her ears had been picked away as she'd fretted by the window, staring outward and waiting to see the cars go by... but they never did. When the sun would go down in the evening each day, she was surprised, as though the whole day hadn't passed at all and it was an illusion.

I'm in shock, she told herself. The diagnosis seemed far away and unreal. However, she couldn't will herself out of the apartment.

Halfway through the third day, Katy admitted something. JD wasn't coming back. He was probably that bloody smudge on the mattress. Since that morning, she had started trying to explain what had happened but hadn't gotten far. For one, if he had exploded, there would be way more goo. Humans had a lot more inside of them than a little puddle like what she'd seen on that mattress. Also... how? People didn't just explode, and neither did rabbits. There *was* no scientific explanation. The question was all that consumed her thoughts.

She counted ideas on her fingers, muttering to herself and flipping through some of the old textbooks she kept on a bookshelf in the corner of her apartment. Like a madwoman, her hair tangled and starting to smell, she wrote down notes in her new field notebook that she had bought to replace the one that was almost full. Formulas and ideas started to take form. In all the possibilities in the universe, perhaps there was some perfect chance of molecules coming together and apart so that people could spontaneously implode? What if there was some understanding of physics and science that scientists hadn't even been able to scratch the surface of, and which could result in something like this? Maybe everything humanity had been doing over the last hundreds of years was building up to a spontaneous event, in some energetic disaster that humanity wasn't yet intelligent enough to detect. She could find nothing, however, and she was frustrated that her colleagues weren't calling or texting her back. Her books were useless.

After some effort, Katy changed out of her dirty clothes. They went into the trash can in the bathroom, she never wanted to see those ratty pajamas again. Sliding into her favorite dirty hiking boots, she walked out the front door, her hair still slightly matted and without its usual raven-feather sheen. The street was quiet as she scanned the neighborhood. After a few deep breaths, she wandered across the street to her neighbor Tim's door. She wasn't so fond of the guy, but he was the only neighbor she'd really ever talked to, so she'd decided she might as well start there. The knock at the door echoed across the apartments and houses, and she waited. And knocked again when no one answered and waited some more. She shifted uneasily, unsure how long she should wait. After a few minutes of pacing at the front door, she tried the handle. She found that the door was unlocked after she gave it a little wiggle. Knowing very well that she was invading someone else's space, she stepped into the entry, trying not to make too much noise in her heavy boots.

"Tim? It's Katy. I just had a weird night... the other night. Did you hear anything crazy, too?" She took off her shoes at the front door—it only seemed polite. The smell of kitchen garbage that needed to be taken out made her nose prickle. Flies spun lazily around the room, gathering mostly near the trash and on his bed. Her heart dropped, swimming around somewhere in her stomach acid as she walked through the small apartment. No one was there, but there was a big red stain on the mattress.

"No, no, no...." Katy leaned up against the wall. "This isn't happening." She kept repeating it to herself, sliding down on the wall to rest on her butt. Her palms pressed to the cool wall like it was a life-float and she'd begun slipping away into the ocean. Her heart was a crashing siren in her throat and chest, pushing against her sternum. Breaths came short and shallow, over and over again; she was hyperventilating. The air was burning down her throat and blackening her lungs, and the panic was making her vision flash black and white.

She fell onto her forearms and vomited. It was a weak, pitiful retch since she had eaten practically nothing. She kept retching for some time. Every time it felt like it was over, she would feel a mouth-watering drive to do it again. Her breath came out in dry sobs as she pushed away from the mess. She pulled out her phone and dialed Tim's number.

Just like JD's phone the other day, a phone vibrated from near the bed, abandoned.

The fish in Tim's elaborate fish tank, which he had always been so proud of, were floating, dead from neglect. One dead fish was hanging in a limp C-shape near the filter, occasionally flipping and spinning as the water gurgled and flowed over it. Fixating on the fish, Katy acknowledged it was the only movement in the room aside from her heaving chest and the lazy spinning flies. She didn't want to look at the stillness elsewhere or let her eyes wander to the red stain that flies were dancing around.

When her stomach stopped rolling every time she moved her head, she climbed to her feet again and stumbled out the front door with her boots half on. Scuffling and dragging her feet along the hot, dry sidewalk, she looked both ways across the empty road and walked up to her car. The interior was hot and stuffy, with dead air that was left over from an entire Summer of being closed up. When she turned the ignition, she got nothing. She tried one more time and then sat there staring out of the windshield. For about five minutes, she roasted in the car, letting the tears dry on her face and tasting the acid taste of vomit in her mouth. Finally, she hauled herself out of the car and opened the backseat, where she kept a self-jumper battery. She hoped it wasn't dead, as well.

The car coughed before starting, but the jumper battery hadn't lost its charge yet. After letting it get a charge, she hopped out, pulled off the cables, and placed the jumper in the back of the car. She pulled away from where she'd been parked next to JD's truck. She didn't know where she would go yet, but just started driving down the middle of the road while looking from side to side. Still not a single person on the street. Then, there, on the sidewalk, was a red splotch. She slowed down to stare at it, a typical rubber-necker staring at an accident on the freeway. And then, suddenly, she sped up in a panic as though the spot would see her staring and think she was rude. Her heart was thundering in her chest for several minutes, and her hands cold and sweaty on the steering wheel. The roller coaster of her heartbeat and emotions had her feeling worn out, like she herself was a battery about to die.

About ten minutes of driving later, she found herself in front of the police station. A row of patrol cars remained neatly parked in front. Pulling up her car at the gap between the cars at the front door, she left it running and climbed out. After peering in the windows and seeing nothing, she tried the door. It swung open, and the air conditioning hit her in the face. She tiptoed into the lobby. No one was there. After hesitating within the lobby, she wandered back into what she thought they called "the bull pen." The officers' desks were neatly lined up. She saw a dark patch on one of the padded office chairs, and turned and ran back to the lobby.

"HELP! HELP, WHERE IS EVERYBODY?!?" she screamed. Her voice cracked—it hurt to yell that loudly. Her voice echoed across the empty room and linoleum floors. Her shoulders slumped as she left the police station.

In the car, tears wet her skin as she drove aimlessly through town. She let them dribble down her rounded cheeks and wrap down her chin. The salt made her face itch and sting, and her vision kept drowning in each tear before it fell. Busy intersections that used to make her nervous were empty, with only leaves and her Subaru blowing across them. The stoplights still worked, blinking through their colors meaninglessly. She stopped at the first red and then ran through the next. What was the point if there weren't other drivers? She pulled up to the grocery store she normally went to, its parking lot empty except for a few cars she guessed had belonged to the overnight stockers. Routine had gotten the best of her and she'd returned to a familiar place.

The sliding glass door opened automatically, ushering her into the echoing space. She pushed a cart and paused at the entryway.

"Hello?" she called out again. Her voice fell against the rows of cereal and canned foods, unanswered.

The coolers and fridges were still on, so she selected meat and all of the fresh vegetables that she could fit in the cart. Pausing by the pastries, she saw a cake that caught her eye. It had bright pink, fluffy frosting on top. Something that she would normally admire and then hurry past. Instead, she picked up the glorious, horrifically pink cake and put it into the cart in the shelf section intended for a child. Her mouth watered a little with her thinking about the sugary, creamy frosting. She'd always had a killer sweet tooth.

She paused. *What if everyone is really gone? What if I'm one of the only people left? How long will the power stay on?* No, that was crazy talk. There had to be a good explanation for where everyone had gone. An earthquake warning had gone out… one serious enough that everyone had evacuated; Katy had just missed it because she'd come down with whatever it was that was plaguing her right now. The thoughts spun around in her mind as she tried to puzzle it all together. Her head and body ached from lack of food and accumulated stress. She noticed that her migraine-like head pain had faded away, however.

"Then why is all the food still here?" She recalled that last year, when there'd been a panic about fires, the shelves had been stripped of everything useful down to the last bottle of water. But now, everything was still neatly in its place, with new special displays stacked up at the end of the rows. Like the night crews had finished setting up for the next day and been about to go home, and no one had touched the store since. Everything seemed in such regular order.

She rolled her shopping cart up to the checkout area and stopped, staring at the row of unmanned checkouts. She had never stolen anything in her life, but the thought crossed her mind. No one was there to stop her, and it was always hard to squeeze by with the salary from the Summer and the small stipend that accompanied her scholarship.

No, she couldn't steal. What if this was some big prank and someone was waiting with cameras outside to shame her for stealing?

She left a wad of cash on the glass of the self-checkout. Keeping the dream of an ultimate prank show in her mind, she prepared herself for the camera crews she imagined would be outside to greet her and congratulate her for playing "The Silent Apocalypse Gameshow." She squeezed her eyes shut after the front doors floated open, waiting for the clapping to start. The wind whispered its laughter to her, and a fat pigeon fluffed up its feathers and cooed as it pursued another pigeon. The parking lot was as empty as it had been when she had gone in. No one celebrated her purchase. Just a horny pigeon and the early Autumn breeze.

She carted her food over to the car, tossing it all in the back haphazardly. Except for the cake; the cake, she gingerly carried to the front seat and set on the floor of the passenger side so that it wouldn't slide around. As she drove, she would glance down at the cake to make sure that her driving wasn't causing it to slide around and mess up the frosting.

She ate the cake first when she got home. Cutting a modest piece and placing it on its own plate, she sat facing the wall at her small kitchen table. She bit into the first piece, then licked the fluffy frosting off of the fork. So sugary, you could almost crunch down on the individual sugar granules. Her mouth watered at the sweetness she normally didn't allow herself. Then, bite by bite, her piece of cake disappeared, and she cut another, then another. Half of the cake was gone by the time she stopped. The sugar in her bloodstream buzzed around and her headache improved even more.

"HEY, HEY, HEY!" The old dog was at it again, barking his hoarse, half-mute bark. Usually, the owners brought him inside for at least part of the day, but he'd been left outside since... *it* had happened. He had his face pressed against the glass of her back door, so close that he left wet dog-nose smears as he wagged his tail back and forth.

Katy sighed and pushed away from her cake feast to rip open the bag of dog food that she'd taken from the store.

"Here you go, you old fart," she told him as she opened the door. The dog wagged its tail furiously as she set down a heaping soup bowl full of dog food.

"I wonder...." She climbed down her back stairs and through the gate she had left open between the yards and hopped up onto the neighbor's deck. She knocked on the back door. No answer. She tried to open it, but it was locked. Looking around, she found a fake rock by the back door with a key underneath it.

Walking into the stuffy, dark room, she recognized the smell immediately. The same smell of the sidewalk squirrel from last week, when life had seemed a lot safer and simpler. She flipped on the light and walked into the bedroom.

"Yep, there you are, Mr. and Mrs. Walker," she said, the two red-brown spots of gristle on the bed staring back at her. She flipped off the light.

"I guess no one is here to take care of Fido anymore."

She walked outside and looked at the gap in the lattice of the deck where the dog had been hiding when she'd first come to see him. Just then, he ran up to her, smacking his lips from his meal and wagging his tail like a helicopter.

The panic and sadness she had been feeling earlier had turned into a dullness that spread across her entire world.

She tried to focus on the scruffy old lab-mix in front of her, to not let her mind spiral into panic again.

"What did they call you anyway?" He ran out of the gate and then back toward her a few times, still wagging his tail like a madman.

"Well, you don't have a collar on you, old dog... yeah, Old Dog. I'll just call you that." Old Dog didn't seem to have any complaints about his new name and trotted out into the neighborhood with his light brown tail high—like a flag of freedom.

"At least someone is having fun."

She put her hands into her pockets and went back inside her own home, leaving the back door cracked and all of the yard gates open so that the dog could come in if he wanted.

LET ME OUT

The husky was hungry. Not madness hungry yet, but hungry enough that the sensation was beginning to burn deep in his stomach, chewing away at him from the inside. He clawed desperately at the chain-link fence with his front paws, the sound rattling across the gravel yard. *Let me out.* He paced back and forth along the fence. His pen was beginning to smell strongly of his urine. Usually, they came and cleaned up his pen every other day. The husky used to be a house pet when he'd been a sweet little puppy.

Tucker remembered when he'd come home to his family. It had been Winter and Christmas, and they had welcomed him with open arms. He'd been in love. Then, he'd gotten bigger and the teenage children hadn't liked his teeth and his accidents on the floor.

They didn't have time for him. He was left in the backyard.

After he'd begun escaping and digging up the lawn, a new outbuilding had been constructed at the very edge of the property. A prison where he couldn't ruin anything nice. That's where he had lived the last two years. At first, they'd taken him out for walks about once a week. Then, they'd done that less and less.

Whining desperately, Tucker dug at the gap between the fence and the concrete that was closest to the main house. Why hadn't they come for him? Every day, he looked forward to when his people would come trudging across the lawn with a bowl of food and the hose for fresh water. They would talk to him while he bounced wildly up and down, barking out his excitement. It had been days since he'd had fresh water, food. *Trapped.* Their arrival was his only relief from his solitude.

Please come back.

He didn't understand what he'd done wrong to be trapped here like this. One of his claws tore as he dug at the hard ground, leaving a streak of desperate blood across the already soiled concrete.

He stopped his pawing for a moment to look out the other side of his pen. The road that he normally spent his day watching was silent. No cars drove by on the highway for him to yell out to. One semi-truck was over-turned on the side of the road, a corpse. It had crashed on the night he had heard the sound. *The screaming.* At first, he had leaped up from his tiny plastic doghouse to bark at the singing coyotes. Then, he'd realized it wasn't the coyotes coming onto his territory. The screaming had been coming from the house. Then, when the sound had gotten so great that Tucker had whimpered and tucked his tail between his legs, the truck had gone diving off the side of the road. With that final crash, all had fallen silent again. The spinning tires of the truck had slowed, and he'd been alone.

He desperately wanted to get to the house, to help his people. What had happened to them? But he was in his pen. Forgotten.

He turned away from the road and back to his empty water bowl. He dragged his dry pink tongue across the tangy metal of the bottom of the dish. Wishing for even a drop of water. There was none. Then to his food bowl. He licked up one crumb that he had missed, from the ground beside his bowl, one fleck of flavor for his rumbling stomach. The panic began to rise in his chest. The only way he had stayed sane was by being able to see his people twice a day, their daily routine being the only thing that had kept him from losing his spirit.

He tilted his white and gray muzzle to the sky and howled. The mournful sound bounced off of the farmhouse and back to him, then across the flat plains. There was no reply. He had to get out. He had tried before to escape and had failed, but now there was a desperation inside of him. He knew he would die if he did not get out.

With a renewed fervor, he bit at the chain-link fence with his teeth. Blood filled his mouth as he tore at and shook the metal. The only thing that gave way was the soft tissue of his gums and tongue. He shook his head and let the blood spray and foam from his lips. At least it was moisture on his parched tongue. He charged the doghouse, leaping on top and scrabbling for purchase on the slanted plastic roof. For a moment, he thought he would fall back to the ground, but he managed to gather his legs beneath him. A husky, he was made for athletic feats. He was made to run and pull and dash through deep snow. He looked at the one gap between the tin roof and the chain-link. He had tried before, but now was the time. He would get out.

His muscles coiled and prepared, his bright-blue eyes on the prize. With one motion, he was launching himself through the air, his claws extended. Initially, he was able to cling to the top corner, and then he lost purchase. With his paws flailing out in all directions, he fell onto the concrete, hard. Yelping out in pain, he limped up to his feet. The fall didn't deter him, though; he climbed again, and again.

The floor of the concrete pen was no longer covered only in dirt and his excrement; it was covered in his blood and fur, too. His sides heaved and he panted weakly. One more time. *This time.* He knew it was this time. Instead of climbing atop the doghouse, he jumped into the corner. Another jump to the other side. *Higher, higher.* He knew it was his last try before he fell to the ground to die in this prison. The gap was right there. With the last bit of his strength, he pushed off the corner where he had climbed the chain-link. His head smashed against the tin roof and he managed to pop his head and front paws through. Luckily for him, his family had done a poor job at roof security. They'd never expected him to climb this high and had placed the sheet of metal on top without securing it. His hind legs dangled, and he kicked to find the fence to push off of. With a groan, he managed to squeeze his shoulders out, as well, and then his chest. Finally, his tail and back end were bunched at the top of the cage, and he looked down at the dry grass of freedom. He leaped down to the ground, falling into a heap. The roof clattered shut as he squeezed free.

Tucker stood up on his trembling legs and looked into his prison. *I got out.*

He tested the air around him with his cracked dry nose. He followed his burning urge for food and water, and he followed his desperate need for his people. Around the side of the house, he found a bucket that had collected rainwater near the shed. With desperate slurps, he drank and drank, stomach pumping as he filled it with fresh water. He drank so fast and desperately that, when he stepped away from the pail, he threw it all up immediately because his stomach had been so shocked by the cool water. He dove back to the bucket and drank more. This time, it stayed down.

The shed was much easier to break into than his pen had been to break out of. The latch had been only partially closed. He found his food and, within seconds, was crunching down on the dry kibble. Strings of drool roped around his muzzle as he ate.

With his burning needs sated, he trotted up to the back door of the house and whined.

He remembered sitting here countless times before. *Let me in. Let me in, please, I miss you.* He would scratch at the back panels until one of his people would open the door and yell.

"TUCKER, NO! BAD DOG!" they would shout at him while he wagged his tail and tried to pry his way into the kitchen.

He tried scratching now, even though his feet hurt when he did. Like in his pen, he left scrapes of blood across the already dirtied and gouged door. No one came. *Let me in.* He began to bark loudly. If the scratching didn't work, the barking always did.

No one came.

He barked for an hour until his body gave out on him. Then, he curled up on the back mat and fell asleep. In his dreams, he was running with his people in the fields around their home as they laughed and threw a ball for him.

Let me in.

CITY CRUSH

"Danielle?" Katy asked after the beep of the voicemail, pressing the phone hard to her burst eardrums and hoping for a reply to bloom to life through the phone speaker. "Danielle, I fucking miss you and I'm scared." Her last few words had come out with a hiccup. She was sitting on the couch in her underwear, hugging her knees into her chest so hard that her arms and knees were trembling.

She pressed *END* on the call and let the tears fall. Old Dog looked up from where he was resting on the floor with his head on his dirty paws. Katy wiped away the tears. They stung on the raw skin of her face.

Katy had met Danielle when she'd first moved to California. She had taken a day trip to San Francisco, alone, to sightsee. Her parents had just left after helping her pick out an apartment and move in, and she hadn't been sure what to do with herself for the week before classes started. She'd found herself in a coffee shop next to an art gallery and sat down to have a cold drink and rest. As usual, she'd had a notebook with her for doodling. Katy didn't remember exactly what she'd been drawing, but suddenly an iced coffee had appeared next to her right hand. Danielle had invited herself to Katy's table. Next,

Danielle had invited her to come see her art gallery next door, and the rest was history.

Katy remembered the last night she had spent with Danielle before she'd left for Austin for the Summer. The two of them had sat out on Danielle's tiny balcony and drunk at least a bottle and a half of wine. They'd been laughing and relaxing in the cool early-Summer air.

Outside, now, the sun was just rising. The new morning light gave the apartment a blue glow as she sat with the lights off on the couch. She'd woken up in the middle of the night and sat there in a stupor, flipping through the pre-set channels on the TV. She couldn't seem to find any live programs.

"I need to check on Danielle," she said out loud, dropping the remote. She opened her texts with her, looking at the long list of unseen and unanswered messages in outgoing calls. Katy had been dialing the numbers of everyone she knew nonstop. Including Danielle, especially Danielle. The calling had become so obsessive that she'd had to leave her phone plugged in all the time because she was draining the battery so fast.

After eating the last piece of cake, she shrugged on her leather jacket and took the keys from their peg in the narrow entrance hallway. Old Dog trotted along behind her. The air was cool and fresh, the beginning of a gorgeous blue-skied Autumn day. Old Dog tilted his head up to the sky, his eyes squinted shut against the bright sun. Katy did the same, letting the sun warm her tear-stained face. Damn, that felt good. Good enough to eat away at the panic that she was fighting with every breath. She looked around the suburban street. She listened carefully, searching for movement. No one walked by with their dog or hopped into their car to run errands. No children rode their bikes down the quiet street.

Her heart began to pound again at the enormity of her loneliness. Before it could consume her, she unlocked the car and opened the back door to see if the dog would jump in. He did, as though they had been going for rides together his entire life. She watched his hips give out as he jumped, and he struggled to climb into the back seat. He was a very old dog. Too old to be forced to sleep outside in the yard every night like he had been for the last few years that Katy had been living next door. At least she could make sure that, for the rest of his life, he slept on a good bed and had all of the love he could handle. She stroked his soft floppy ears before closing the door and climbing into the driver's seat.

A few minutes later, the freeway was a horrifying ghost town. Katy stopped at the first twisted wreckage she found, putting the car into park and stepping out onto the road. She peeked behind her to make sure no other cars were coming on the three-lane road. A habit, really. The voice in the back of her head reminded her that no car would be coming, ever.

A pick-up truck was smashed into the concrete partition, the entire front of the truck caved in and warped around the solid barrier. She crept forward, standing on her tiptoes to see into what was left of the cab. There was a splatter of blood across the seat and steering wheel. She could see flecks of white on the steering wheel and the seatbelt, which was still plugged in. Reaching out, she touched the sticky mess, plucking one of the white pieces off of the seatbelt. Upon closer examination, she determined it was bone. She tossed it back into the wreckage and hurried back to her car.

The truck wasn't the only wreck she saw. Several other cars had met a similar fate, veering off the road when their owners had lost control in agony or completely disappeared. She wove through them carefully. Luckily, none of them had blocked the road completely as she made her way to the familiar exit she normally took to get to Danielle's neighborhood.

She almost turned around, though. It was much more obvious here that something bad had happened. Something terrible. Her hands quivered on the steering wheel as she passed the wreckage of cars leading into the maze of city buildings. When she was close to Danielle's apartment, she had to back up because a delivery truck and a taxi had crashed into each other, blocking the road. Going up the wrong way on the one-way alley street behind Danielle's place, she stopped on the opposite side of the entrance to the apartment block. She parked in the middle of the road and then sat at the steering wheel trying to calm her panting breath. Old Dog stood up and wagged his tail, staring out the window.

Outside, the slamming of the car door echoed against the brick and steel of the city. It was the only sound.

Her boots on the sidewalk sounded unnaturally loud as she rounded the corner. Old Dog's nails clicking on the concrete made the hair on the back of her neck stand up.

"Okay, Katy, stay calm," she murmured to herself, wiping her sweaty palms on her pants.

The silence was so terrifying. An omission from ordinary life in the city that had turned it into a surreal twilight zone. She begged herself to stay calm, offering it as a repetitive chant in her mind as she found herself sneaking down the street as though she would be caught by a terrible beast if she made too much noise and disturbed the library-quiet of the art district. She crept past the Starbucks on the corner where she and Danielle would sometimes grab a latte before going on a walk together. Despite it being prime coffee-time, the lights were off and the windows were shuttered. The chairs outside on the patio were all neatly placed, with no one sitting outside and enjoying the morning sun.

She walked up to the narrow entrance door for Danielle's apartment building. Danielle's old car was parked at the end of the block. Katy thought Danielle had probably been pretty proud of getting that parking spot for once. But the cheery blue of the old block didn't lift her mood, as she saw a black sedan crashed into the row of parked cars in front. From the sidewalk, looking up, she could see Danielle's window to her living room. She pulled out her phone and called. The phone rang and rang, and once again went to voicemail.

"Danielle? I decided to stop by. Could you let me in?" She winced at the way her voice traveled through the silent city air and hugged herself with her free arm as she paced back and forth at the front steps. Finally, she hung up and sat down on the concrete steps. A light breeze ruffled the trees that were neatly planted on the sides of the street. Movement caught her eye, and she felt a jolt of excitement in her chest as she looked up. Some seagulls drifted over the building on the other side of the street. Only seagulls.

Katy stood up and tried the door. Of course, it was locked. The entryways to apartments in the city were always locked. For good measure, though, she gave it a shake. The door rattled in its frame but didn't budge. She cursed herself for giving back her spare key before she'd gone to Austin that Summer. If she'd had it now… well, she would have been able to find out the truth she didn't really want to know.

"Danielle?" she yelled up to the window that was staring back at her, gloomy and uninterested.

Her voice bounced off of the narrow block. A group of pigeons took flight in surprise at the disturbance. Old Dog poked his head from around the corner where he had been sniffing, pausing to stare at her.

"Danielle, WAKE UP!" She was yelling and crying at the same time, her voice cracked and desperate.

She remembered the many times that she'd come here to visit, and her friend had poked her head out of the window to talk to her before coming downstairs. Katy had always thought it was embarrassing to stand on the busy sidewalk having a conversation in the air while people pushed past her and looked up to see what she was looking at. Now, all she wanted was for Danielle to unlock that shabby window frame and pop her head out and give her classic glittering smile.

"Danielle…." Katy let the tears tumble down her cheeks again. Her hands felt numb. She gave them a shake, but the tingling wouldn't go away. She shook the door handle again.

As a person who used logic as her weapon to cut through most situations, she was currently swinging through the dark at anything that could explain what had happened. Had there been a bomb scare? World War 3? How had she possibly missed the announcements that could have prompted everyone to file out of San Francisco and Berkeley in an orderly fashion and leave her behind with an extremely old dog? Her nose blew a snot bubble, and she used the sleeve of her jacket to wipe at her face uselessly. With snot still stuck to her upper lip, she then began to feel angry. Katy wandered to the edge of the block, where she found a big rock in the landscaping separating the road from the sidewalk. She noticed her fingers looked a little blue as she carried it back to the front door.

She stood on the stoop, unsure if she'd be able to commit to her next move. Frozen, holding a big rock in the middle of the city. With a yell, she raised the rock up and smashed it down on the old-style key lock. It smashed and dented the already scratched copper fixture but didn't break the door open. With another growl, she smashed again. The door rocked on its hinges, and the wood splintered around the lock. Katy saw a glimpse of herself in the reflection of the smudged glass. Her lips were curled up in a snarl, her eyes dark and puffy. For the third time, she smashed at the lock.

"OW!" she yelped, and the lock broke. So did her finger.

In her frenzy, her finger had been in the way of her door attack. She let the stone fall from her hands and bounce down the steps. She crumpled to the ground, clutching her right pointer finger even as blood welled up from the split fingernail, already red and angry. The sight of it made her cry even harder. Her sobs turned into a woofing sound as she sucked air in and out, trying to manage the searing pain from her finger. Old Dog came running at the sound of her sobbing, his tail sweeping low and concerned. He sat staring at her from the bottom of the steps, his dark eyes somber.

"Stupid, stupid, stupid." The pain from her finger didn't subside as she got up and power-walked to her car sitting around the corner. She rummaged around in the back and found the mini first-aid kit that she kept in the back, underneath the shopping bags and loose clothes. There was one package of gauze left. With a fumbling left hand, she unwrapped the fluffy material and covered her finger, hissing in pain as she did. When she let go of her makeshift wrapping, she shook out a few Tylenol from the kit. They were long-expired, but she dry-swallowed them anyway.

After collecting herself, sitting on the trunk of the car and staring down the empty street, she went back to Danielle's apartment building entrance. Before going in, she scooped the stone up and cradled it in her left arm. Squished finger or not, she had a feeling she might need to use it again.

The air inside smelled stale. Like old carpeting and cigarettes. Katy's nose tickled as she stomped up the switchback stairs, panting as she got closer to the fourth floor.

She stood in front of the green door with its neat black entry mat. Like she had hundreds of times before. Setting the rock down, she rapped on the door with the knuckles of her left hand.

"Danielle, I'm here, open up!" Her throat burned when she spoke again, calling out some more. She tried to remember the last time she'd had a drink of water.

She waited. And waited. She knocked again and again. No one came to the door. She turned to the other side of the stairwell and knocked on Danielle's neighbor's door. An old lady who she had said hi to a few times at the mailboxes. No answer. Her legs and arms felt weak and heavy. With her leaden body, she tried both the doors. Locked. She stomped down to the third floor and tried there, as well.

Once she had tried all of the doors on every floor, she ended up back in front of Danielle's. The faded green door with the scratches on it, and the brass peephole. She smashed at the lock, this time being careful to keep her fingers out of the way. The door broke much faster than the downstairs one, and Katy stumbled forward into Danielle's entryway.

"Hello? It's Katy!" She set down the rock next to the neat row of shoes and wandered into the apartment, past the posh art on the walls and the neat furniture. There was a bottle of wine on the kitchen table, and two glasses with hints of red wine at the bottom. Katy felt embarrassed. Maybe Danielle had company.

And she did have company. When Katy turned the corner of the small one-bedroom apartment, she saw her. Well, what was left of her and some poor guy. On Danielle's soft linen sheets were two red-brown stains.

"No," she said, breathless. "Please. Please, no." She clutched her injured hand and stared.

"I can't... I just...." She turned and sprinted out of the apartment, knocking into a console table as she fled. A vase tumbled off and shattered across the worn wooden floor. She didn't look back; she just kept running. Her feet pounded down the stairs, and she burst out the battered door downstairs. Old Dog, who had very slowly climbed the stairs up to the apartment, had elected to rest on the landing of the stairway instead of going into the apartment with her. Old Dog tried to keep the pace as she left, limping behind her. She didn't stop until she was leaning against her old Subaru, gasping for breath. Old Dog caught up to her and sat patiently next to the back door. She opened it for him and got behind the wheel.

Driving back home in a daze, she weaved between the crashed cars. When she got home, she took off all of her clothes and fell into her stained bed, cradling her broken finger.

SPINNING OUT

Seven days later, the water stopped running. Katy had gone on two expeditions around the neighborhood to view the red spots, as she called them. Still, there was no sign of another person. She had written some large signs with her address and "ALONE PLEASE HELP" on them, though, and posted them at some big intersections across town.

That evening around 9 p.m., the power went out also. Katy was sitting on the back porch drinking a beer when it happened. She rarely drank alone, but it seemed appropriate. It was the end of the world and she might as well have a beer. The lights in her apartment behind her went off with a final tick. She sighed and got up from her chair, spinning a little bit from the alcohol. She didn't need to look in a mirror to know her cheeks were flushed red, as they always did when she drank. She flicked roughly at the light near the back door. Nothing happened. She set down her drink and went to the power panel, where she flipped at the switches. Nothing happened.

Standing there in the darkness, Katy realized that she was really in trouble. She couldn't sit and eat cake forever because no one was making new cakes. No one at the public services office was maintaining the power, and no one was going to serve up new steaks in the deli. If she didn't figure out how to live on her own, she was going to die. Be a red splotch.

Though, she figured her time for exploding into a little blob was over, and she would go the slow way now.

Standing there with her hand still pressed against the power switches, she trembled. Alone... this alone? What if it was just this town? Still, what now? If there was no work to go to, no papers to write and no landlord to pay rent to, what was there? The room began to spin a bit, and it wasn't just from the beer. She went back out to the porch to watch the setting sun and let the gravity of the situation sink in. Sitting there, she fiddled with the makeshift splint on her crushed finger. The nail was black, and the flesh of her finger showed a patterning of purple, green, and blue. The swelling had gone down over the last week and she could bend it, but the fingernail looked ready to fall off. She sat on the deck with her legs dangling down until the sun had slipped beyond the horizon and the last glow of light had left. In the dimness of twilight, she crawled onto the couch and cried herself to sleep.

With blankets piled high, the phone that was about to die finally fell loose out of her hand. She let sleep settle over her, a second pile of soft blankets.

She was standing in her childhood home just outside of Portland. It was Autumn there, too, tree colors rich with the expectation of Winter. She was naked, walking through *the halls of the big house of her childhood. Feet silent on the hardwood floors. Looking down at her toes made her head spin, so she kept her eyes forward. Maybe the world **was** spinning, it was hard to tell. She rested her hand on the wall for support as she walked.*

"Momma?" she called out.

"Mom, I'm home from Cali!" She walked out to the back, imagining her mom tending to the last harvest of her garden before the frost came. She walked outside, and all that met her was a big red spot. Next to it were the trimming shears and a pile of vegetables that had been freshly plucked from the garden. The husks of corn sitting on the bricks were splattered with blood.

Katy's eyes opened, her back aching from the plush couch. She rustled the blankets around her and noticed that she could hear a bit better. To avoid breaking down into tears, she continued to rustle the blankets, listening to the sound that was much louder than it would have been the day before.

"I am the last person on Earth." She kicked her blanket off of herself. "I'm completely alone."

She knew it to be true. Like a bear knows to fatten up in the Autumn and go to sleep in the Winter. She knew it like a tiny kangaroo Joey, only a pink eraser compared to what it would grow to be, knew to climb up to its mother's pouch, blind and helpless. Sometimes animals just knew these things, because it was in their very biology. This was the first time Katy had truly felt lonely since the night it had happened, though. In the early, still-dark morning hours, she hugged her blankets closer and shivered. Alone, in the dark and unable to fall back asleep. The early hours left the room blue and empty as she stared at the wall, shivering. She was used to sleeping alone, but at this moment, she ached to hear the breathing of someone else. Something to stop the muffled silence that she was being subjected to. Anything to chase away the walls pressing in. Her head had a vice grip of a headache around her temples, and her knuckles ached from squeezing the blankets so hard.

She sat up, listening to the empty world. If she had been a bat, her wide ribbed ears would have been rotating endlessly, listening to every chirp and creak the world offered up. She rubbed her thumbs over the blankets, trying to ground herself to what she could touch and sense right now instead of the emptiness outside.

Then, in the blue darkness of late night, she heard something. A scrabbling, dragging sound outside the windows. Her fingers tensed on the blankets, and she hauled them farther up her body. She glanced down to see if Old Dog heard it, too. He was deep asleep, his chest rising and falling. A collision of something black and alive thumped against the outside of the building, darkening the windows completely and throwing her into pitch blackness. The thing outside pulled and heaved at the windows and the door… dark smoke was trying to pry its way into any crack it could. Small tendrils wound their way through small holes and gaps in the door, like clawed hands trying to make purchase on the hardwood floors and the walls to pull themselves all the way in. Katy sat in silent terror for what felt like hours as the smoke wailed to be let inside.

As suddenly as it had come, the shadow dissipated and left her alone to tremble beneath the sheets. Katy wondered if it had been another nightmare.

A few hours later, Katy woke up from the weak, tepid sleep she'd managed after hours of lying awake in fear of whatever had come knocking. Gasping, she looked toward the windows. The soft morning light greeted her cheerfully, and Old Dog's tail thumped on the hardwood as she sat up. He licked her exposed hand and blinked slowly up at her.

Feeling battle-worn, Katy stroked his soft ears as she thought.

She had to find out what had happened, and she had to find other people. And fight off the insanity that she imagined was creeping in through the windows and doors of her mind. Was she being hunted?

"Now what, huh?" Old Dog didn't reply, just looked up at her with his mouth wide open, tongue flopping to one side. He had white fur framing his amber face. The light reflected on his dark brown eyes, showing a glimmer of cataracts. The hot breath on her face from his panting tongue was old and rotten, and she could see that he was missing several of his teeth. The rest were yellow, some of them so rotten that they were almost brown, and all of them were worn down to stumps. She leaned away from his awful breath and lay back down, nestling her head deep into the pillows.

A few minutes later, a rumbling in her stomach forced her out of bed. She scrounged around in the kitchen, peering into the now-warm fridge. A few pieces of cheese were flung into Old Dog's eagerly waiting mouth. He smacked his lips and wagged his tail furiously as Katy found some stale bread and spread the now-soft butter over them. She sat in the soft blue light of morning, her eyebrows knitted together as she thought and chewed on her meager meal.

"I need some air." Katy took her keys from the hook next to the door.

Old Dog spun in a circle, bouncing on his old feet. "HEY, HEY, HEY!" he barked his hoarse bark, tongue lolling out to one side. The keys were the walk-time sound. Katy reached down and ruffled his soft ears, a slight smile curling the corner of her mouth. It was good to have a dog around again—she missed her parents' hounds desperately.

For a moment, things felt peaceful instead of lonely as she strolled down the street with her hands stuffed in her pockets. The sound of Old Dog's toenails clicking on the concrete was a comfort. He walked close to her heel, matching her pace except to stop and smell the grass. The air was crisp and clean… the cleanest she had likely ever breathed in Berkeley. No wafts of cigarette smoke from someone walking a few yards ahead of her to tickle her nose; no car fumes. The factories outside of town were dark, and the cars weren't driving. Animals were exploring the streets more actively, probably curious about where all the noise had gone, just like she was. Katy saw front yards covered with birds, deer weaving between manicured lawns, and even the tail end of what she guessed was a fox. The season was still changing, and birds passed overhead (going in the correct direction this time), heading just a little farther South to pass the Winter.

Her feet brought her to campus. Stopping short at the entrance to her old lab, she remembered something, her eyes going wide.

"The rabbits!" She rushed to unlock the door and went down to JD's old lab. The smell was distinct. Rabbit excrement, and death. She tried the lights. Luckily, they still worked, because there were no windows in the room. The university must have been on a separate power grid from her apartment. At least, she thought that was how the power worked.

"Oh, I'm so sorry," she said to the rabbits. Many of them were already dead from dehydration. A few other cages also had "red spots" left instead of rabbits. Just like the spots she had found elsewhere, all they contained was pooled blood and the odd chunk of tissue. These were the only animal deaths she had seen from the phenomenon. The rabbits that were left wiggled their noses and backed away from the front of the cages. The light was unfamiliar to them after days left in the basement's darkness. All of the rats were dead.

"So, why did you guys die?" She peered into the cages of spots.

Old Dog sniffed curiously, drooling.

"Don't, Old Dog, those rabbits are pumped full of all sorts of shit you don't want," she said, waving him away. The dog ignored her and kept sniffing, his floppy ears perked forward and his tail held erect. A rabbit in the bottom cage cowered against the back wall away from him.

"Chemicals... the rabbits are full of human pharmaceuticals!" Katy said as she realized a possible connection in all this madness. She would go through JD's research once she helped the poor rabbits.

She wasn't going to leave them here to die slowly, alone. Even though she realized that she was also going to die slowly, alone. Shaking the dark thought out of her head, she gave the living rabbits water and food, which they eagerly gobbled up. She figured they were less likely to eat each other if she fed them before putting them in boxes to carry them outside. She had seen rabbits do that before—eat each other. All it took was a little bit of hunger or stress and they would tear into each other like piranhas. She shuddered at the image. The scene of seeing a white rabbit with red around its mouth, with chunks of its old best friend next to it, was something she never wanted to see again. Unfortunately, working near this lab had exposed her to that situation several times.

There were only ten rabbits remaining alive. She carefully carried the thumping boxes full of bunnies upstairs. While holding Old Dog back, she dumped the boxes over in the grass. White fluffs scattered across the university lawn, hopping wildly. They looked like dandelion puff blown about and spinning off into the wind. Scattering in every direction in a dance the wind made. It was possibly the first time these rabbits had seen real grass and sunlight. They had spent their entire existence in that lab, without feeling grass beneath their feet. She sat down, still holding onto Old Dog. He strained against her, whining and pointing toward the rabbits. She waited till they were all long gone before getting up again and letting Old Dog go to chase after their scents.

Then, there was one last trip to be made down into the basement lab.

She went through the papers on JD's desk. As she started to flip through them, her heart ached. *Oh, JD.* They hadn't been extremely close, but he'd been good. Just all around a good guy, and she had enjoyed their lab friendship. And maybe there'd been something more? It was hard to tell with all the other shit going on, but she'd liked having him over that night. Well, before everything had gone sideways. She remembered his hand covering hers as they'd sat on the back deck. It made her chest ache.

She took JD's papers from the desk and walked home with her arms full of coffee-stained notebooks. She thought about JD as she walked, with his broad, generous smile and even broader shoulders. She thought about how warm and solid he had felt under her until...

well, until it had happened. She let some tears fall down her cheeks, brushing them off the top of the stack of papers when they fell. Maybe in another world, another time when she hadn't been so closed off and angry, JD would have been a good lover. The thought made her stomach ache. Old Dog came out of the nearby bushes wagging his tail proudly, interrupting her thoughts. She wiped her tears away and gave him a hearty pat on the side, which he arched into while looking up at her adoringly. His sweet canine affection only made her heart ache more. It was a fierce contrast to the way she had felt about romantic relationships in general, and despite the comfort Old Dog was offering, everything hurt.

Curled up at her kitchen table lit with candles, Katy began to read JD's research. She probably should have kept one of the rabbits for further tests, but she couldn't imagine making one of those animals endure a cage again. She cursed herself for choosing such a theoretical strain of biology. Ecology was great and all—understanding the models of how ecosystems functioned and modeling the growth of populations—but it couldn't help you understand why all humans and some rabbits all went "pop" in the middle of the night.

The rabbits had been used in initial animal trials of cell transfusion. The goal of the tests had been to see if animals could be used to grow organs to replace the failing organs in people. She had noticed that all of the living rabbits had been in the far-right corner of the lab, away from the one that had originally exploded on her.

Medical tests of this nature typically started with rabbits and rats because humans considered them expendable. She hated that. *We could do better. We, as humans, are capable of more.* At least, Katy thought so, and so had JD. That was why he'd cried his way through dissections and thrown up in the trashcan whenever something had gone wrong and the rabbits had ended up with terrible deformities.

The trial Katy read about now was in its early stages, but Katy was surprised to read in the notes that the rabbits in the cages she'd set free had been the control group. Untouched by the rather invasive procedure, they were kept to compare to the rabbits who'd recently been having some of their organs painfully prepped to be removed and cultured with human cells. She wrinkled her nose at the idea and a deep line furrowed its way between her fine eyebrows. Even though she had some insight into what made those rabbits "people-like," what had happened still didn't make any sense. She scribbled down her own notes, pausing idly during the process to doodle a rabbit on the edge of one of the papers. Drawing let her mind wander and explore new ideas.

A few minutes later, she stopped and looked down at what she had drawn: a round-rumped rabbit sitting in a lab cage. The pink-eyed type with downy white fur and a wiggly pink nose. The drawing looked like it was missing something. She added a human ear to its back, poking out naked and fleshy among the plush fur. *Horrible.* She flipped the page over before the illustration could begin bounding across the pages, its grotesque flapping ear listening to her thoughts.

A few days later, the electricity was gone everywhere she explored—a relic of the past now. Several times in the last few days, she had walked into a room and flicked at the switch. The habit would die soon. Amazingly, she still had service on her phone, although she expected that would soon be gone, too. That morning, when she'd gone to start her car to do her loops around the neighborhood—searching for signs of life and charging her phone—she'd seen the gas needle sitting dangerously close to the big red "E." She'd sighed, remembering that she hadn't left much gas in it before she'd left for the Summer. Turning around, she'd driven toward the closest gas station.

About thirty minutes later, she was kneeling on the hard pavement of the gas station, her phone in hand with instructions on how to siphon gas. She stared out at the sea of parking lots and shopping centers across the street. She'd used to hate coming to this gas station because it had been a pain to turn left into it with all of the shopping traffic nearby. So much gray, so much fake. All of this had been something else once and had been paved over to accommodate cars and big grocery stores. Seeing it all empty was disturbing—the ant's nest was beginning to crumble while all the ants were gone. The constant presence of people was what had kept places like this looking like paved-over tombs. Now, she supposed they were tombs. Tombs for all of the little red spots. At least there wasn't a whole world's worth of rotting bodies to smell.

Movement caught her eye as she was finishing up with the fourth canister. The smell of gasoline was stinging her nose and making her eyes water. A flash of red ran across the parking lot. She shot to her feet, tense through her whole body. From around the corner of the lot, a fox poked out its wedge-shaped head. She relaxed. The fox stared at her for a long time with inquisitive green eyes, looking at her like she was an alien. Katy smiled. She had always loved getting a chance to see the wild side of the world. Satisfied that she wasn't a threat, the fox trotted toward the supermarket with its head low, sniffing the ground. Old Dog barked at it from the car where he had been napping. Katy hushed him with a light tap on the window and finished up siphoning gas from the station.

DOG YEARS IN A GALLERY

Another week went by before Katy could comprehend it. Even with her phone to keep track, time seemed to move at a different pace now. The swelling of her crushed finger had gone down, but she'd lost the fingernail. She kept the raw nail bed protected with a band-aid. Time was simultaneously slow and racing. Tasks that would have been an easy errand were now a journey, and Katy was hungry. Now, walking back from a scavenging session at the grocery store, Katy adjusted the heavy bags in her arms to relieve the biting pain from the bag's strap digging into her shoulder. She cursed herself for saying it would be healthier to walk to the store than to drive. Old Dog padded along next to her, stopping to pee on a building or to smell bushes. Occasionally, she would have to slow down till he caught up; he really was an old dog, and his fastest pace was a labored jog. His breath came out in huffing wheezes if he got too excited or had to jog to catch up too often. Watching the way he walked, she guessed that he had arthritis. Every step caused his body to sway, and he had a limp.

"Friday night, Old Dog. Oh, what would I be getting up to on a Friday night a few months ago?" she asked him, re-adjusting the weight again.

"I guess not much, honestly. I didn't like going out." She chuckled to herself. Old Dog looked up at her, blinking his big brown eyes at her in a dog's version of "I love you."

"You know what, let's go out tonight. Out on the town—it will be fun." She patted his head and hurried home, a spring in her step.

After wolfing down a can of beans heated up on a camp stove on the back deck, Katy combed through her closet. The space was dusty, full of clothes she didn't wear. Her wardrobe had always been practical, and she usually loathed having to wear restrictive professional clothing. To her, clothes were to protect and keep her warm, and it annoyed her that everyone else seemed to disagree. She wasn't immune to the charm of a woman wearing a little black dress and sparkling heels, though, and could never tell if she wanted to be her or be with her. In the past, she'd sometimes wandered into a department store and held up such a dress to herself so that she could look in the mirror, only to hurry away when a store attendant came up to help her.

Katy imagined that they were about to go on an elaborate night out—to meet Danielle, who'd always had some fancy studio opening or another she'd be inviting Katy to. Mostly, she'd politely declined. The invitations she'd really hoped for had been when Danielle asked her to come to the studio after it closed. On those nights, the two of them would sip the expensive champagne left over from the guests and critique the art on their own.

She pawed through her clothes, not finding anything that made her light up. She sat on the couch for a minute, looking around the dim apartment. "I know, Old Dog, let's go shopping. Maybe I'll hate it less now that everything is free."

Old Dog looked up at her from the cool tiles of the kitchen and sighed.

The mall was about a twenty-minute drive from her house. She drove into the empty parking lot and pulled right up to the automatic doors at the front. She opened the passenger side door for Old Dog to jump out. Watching him struggle with the action, she knew it wouldn't be long before she would have to lift him out of the car instead of letting him jump. Her heart ached a bit. For so little time, she'd had his companionship, and she was greedy for every moment more of it. The creeping knowledge that he probably wouldn't be around for much longer was almost too much to bear. Taking her mind off of the dreadful thought, she pried open the mall doors and held them open for Old Dog to follow her. He trotted through and wagged his tail as if to say "Thanks."

He was the main reason she hadn't beelined for her parents' house already. That, and the thought that she would go home to two blotches of red. At this point, she had discovered enough red dots and no humans. No, she wasn't ready. That would truly mark the end for her. Better to stay here and take care of Old Dog. He needed her right now.

Her footsteps echoed on the high-traffic tile flooring. At first, she thought about turning around; the skylight in the huge building wasn't letting in much light, and it felt so lonely that the feeling threatened to crush her. She willed herself to keep going, however—there was nothing in here that was going to get her except for her own fears. After her heart slowed down to a normal pace, she urged herself to experience the emptiness fully. How sound moved through the large open space. The mall felt both open wide and crushing at the same time, its air dry and stale from being left undisturbed. Many of the stores were shadowy and dark, without windows to light them up. She pulled a flashlight out of her pocket and walked into a designer store. She had never gone into a store like this one before. The feeling that the shop owner would spot her empty wallet like they had X-ray vision and follow her around like she was a thief had been too overpowering—that, or the guilt that she'd known she would never buy anything had kept her away.

Old Dog found a display of fancy sweaters and laboriously climbed up, making a huffing sound as he curled his tail to his nose in a donut shape. Katy giggled at the idea of bristly gold dog hair all over those expensive sweaters. Her hands ran across the racks of clothing, touching the fabrics and letting the dresses sway on their hangers. In her mind, the room was lit up again with glaring overhead lights instead of her meager flashlight. She imagined that she was a posh middle-aged woman, looking over the clothes with a judgmental eye.

Pulling out a sleek, backless dress, she held it up against her figure. She set the flashlight on top of a display so she could see, and then threw off her clothes in a pile on the ground. Hesitating, she looked at herself naked in the long mirrors outside of the changing rooms. A stranger looked back at her, with eyes that had dark circles under them. She shuddered and looked back to the dress, pulling it over her head. The fabric slid against her skin, hugging tight against her tummy and hips as she shimmied it down to her thighs.

She admired herself, turning this way and that. It was amazing how a piece of fabric could make you feel so different. Her heart tugged in excitement at the idea of showing a dress like this off. Old Dog didn't seem interested in moving as she gathered up her pants and shirt and strolled over to a shoe store to complete her outfit. Her bare feet made small pattering sounds on the cool floor.

Thirty minutes later, a rock slammed through the window of the art studio. Katy smiled a bit, standing in front of the shattered glass in her high heels and her posh dress with another rock in her hand. The pieces of glass crunched under the blanket she laid across the window as she stepped into the dark building. Old Dog hesitated at the entry and then jumped over the shattered doorway. Katy fumbled with the lighter she'd brought, finally getting the wheel to roll, and the dark room jumped to life. She lit a bag full of candles, carefully kneeling down in her high heels and placing them on the floor around the gallery. She wished Danielle could be there with her—she thought that her friend would have found the whole thing terribly poetic. Plus, this was her gallery, after all. She imagined her laughing.

"Darling, you would be the last woman on Earth," she would say, cocking her hip to the side. "You're spiteful enough to outlive all of us!"

"You're so mean sometimes, Dani," Katy would say back, sticking out her tongue.

"You and all the animals, and no more people to piss you off! Ha! Are you sure *you* weren't the one who killed all of us?" Danielle might have replied.

The paintings hanging on the clean white walls of the studio were rich oil paintings of flowers. Danielle would have been complaining about how many artists painted boring flower-vaginas. Of course, she would have completely changed her tune when the artist had come over, preening. Katy smiled at the thought and popped open the champagne she had brought with her. The warm, fizzy bubbles tickled her throat and she coughed, strolling around the small gallery in her heels. The candles flickered light against the lush paintings. Katy reached out and ran her fingers over the thick paint, feeling the hills and valleys that the artist had only intended be seen and not touched. She could imagine Danielle's scream of horror if she had done this in the real world, touching a painting. Now, they were all hers, and she could do what she wanted with them. Her feet started to hurt in the impractical shoes.

She spent an hour wandering through the small gallery, touching the paintings and eventually sitting on one of the benches in the middle of the room. She could feel the tingle of the champagne now and ran an absent hand over Old Dog's warm head.

"Miss you, Danielle." She raised her glass to the huge painting her friend probably would have hated.

Daintily, she blew out the candles scattered about the gallery and stepped over the broken glass again. She drove home slowly and with the windows down, letting the cold air tickle her arm as she rested it outside the window. The stars above were sharp pin-points in the pitch-black sky. The way they'd used to be, before light pollution. Her car was the only prick of light weaving through the jumble of buildings and steep hills of San Francisco. Mostly, cars were neatly parked in parking spots, but there were some that had crashed into each other or into buildings, which slowed her progress through more congested areas. She guessed that most people had been sleeping on the West Coast when *it* had happened. The chaos would have been much worse if it had been rush hour.

Later, she tucked herself into her nest on the couch. Old Dog wheezed and hummed his dog dreams at her feet. She wiggled her toes against his rough fur before drifting off to sleep.

HAUNTED

Her body was drenched in sweat, hair plastered to her forehead and the back of her neck. Katy gasped, flinging the blankets off and blinking in the bright morning light.

She'd had a nightmare about walking downtown San Francisco in the middle of the night, and something following her through the empty streets. Every time she'd turned to look at the thing, it would vanish, so she'd only seen a blur out of the corner of her eye. As she'd become more and more panicked, the thing had also gotten closer. She'd banged on doors and screamed for help, but no one had come. *No one would come.* She'd begun to sprint through the streets, dodging past trashcans and weaving among the parked cars. She'd see tendrils of black smoke lashing out at her, and when she'd turned to swat them away, they would fade into nothingness again.

She wiped sticky sweat from her forehead. Something was different. The apartment was unnaturally quiet. Over the last few weeks, she had grown used to Old Dog plodding over to her when she awoke. They had developed quite the routine over the last few months. Now, after the January semester would have started, their partnership felt like it had been there her whole life. Every morning, his nails would click on the wood flooring and he would begin to pant and wag his tail, breathing his hot rotten-teeth breath on her. Brows furrowed, she looked around for her scruffy old dog.

"Old Dog? Come." She stood up, looking at the back door where he would often sleep.

There was a tawny lump there, but he didn't look up at her when she called.

"Old Dog, hey!" she called more loudly.

He was unnaturally still. She stared, realizing that she could barely see his chest rise and fall.

"Shit!" She scrambled over to his side and placed her hand on his chest. He was alive, but he didn't look good. A bit of foam had collected at the corner of his lip, and his breaths were shallow and half-hearted. After she'd shaken him, his eyes crawled open, and he gave her a weak wag that thumped against the floor like the most tired drummer. His fur looked like old soiled straw and felt just as brittle. She noticed he had a yellow puddle drying around his haunches. He had peed himself in his sleep.

"Hey, hey, hey, old guy. You gave me a scare. What is happening to you?" Katy wished that she could take him to a vet. Peeking at the color of his gums, she saw they looked a bit pale. She remembered the vet doing that with her dogs when she'd been growing up. She didn't know what else she could check, or what to do.

She got up and went to the kitchen, getting out a package of cheese. Old Dog usually loved cheese and would come running if she opened a package. Katy waited, but he didn't come. She brought the cheese back to him and broke up a crumble, holding it in front of his dry and cracked nose. At first, he didn't take it, and her heart ached. Then, his eyes widened and his mouth opened in slow motion. He licked up the morsel. Then another. After the third piece, he heaved himself up to his front paws. Katy stood and lured him to his feet. He shook weakly and wagged his tail, looking up at her.

"Oh, you poor old thing," Katy said as she sprinkled more cheese on the floor for him to lick up.

There was a sound at the door, and Katy jumped and yelped, dropping the chunk of cheese still in her hands. Old Dog bent slowly to lap up the pieces that had fallen from her fingers. Katy hunched down and crept toward the door, hiding behind the dining room table. There, yes, there was definitely something there. A shadow, a flicker, visible through the frosted glass panel. Katy gripped the leg of a chair and hunkered down lower, holding her breath in her throat until her mouth and chest burned.

"It was just a cloud crossing over the sun," she whispered to herself. "Don't be so paranoid."

Old Dog lay back down in his same spot after sniffing the puddle of his own urine. She could hear his wheezing breathing from where she crouched. Katy stole a glance back to watch him. As he lowered himself to the ground, she could see his elbows sway out and tremble. His body looked stringy, like his bones were held together by weakening threads.

A flicker of shadow caught her eye again, and she crouched lower. Barely audible, there was a clicking and a scratching sound coming from the entryway. Katy concentrated on the door, holding her breath. Something slithered up from the small gap under the door—the same gap she had complained to the landlord about and which still hadn't been fixed. It looked like a clawed fingernail. *No, wait. A tendril of smoke.* She squinted to see it while her heart threatened to stampede her. It was gone. The clouds covering the sun were blown away by a strong wind and then only sunlight filtered through the front door.

Katy waited there, frozen in time until she mustered up the courage to walk toward the door. As she stood, her knees popped audibly, and she ducked down again and winced. Nothing happened. Walking on tiptoe, she willed herself toward the front door. She had to see… she had to check. She had to prove to herself that there was nothing there, that there had been nothing there. She crossed from the dining table to the kitchen, once again hiding against the wall. Still no sound or change in the entryway. Biting her lip hard, she turned and walked down the short narrow entryway. Her hand trembled as it gripped the cool doorknob. With fingers shaking, she turned the handle and opened the door.

With owl-wide eyes, she cracked the door to see out. Looking down at where the shadow had been, she gasped. Torn to pieces, with maggots making the last flap of fur of its stomach rise and fall, was what was left of the dead squirrel. Mostly a skeleton now. The one that she had seen on the sidewalk months ago, rotting in the sun. Only a few tufts of fur were left on the bones and insides. Katy took a step back and covered her nose with her hand. That smell. Even after so long, the smell was overpowering.

She looked around the sidewalk, peering toward the side of the house. Nothing else stirred outside. The sun shined down and the breeze moved the trees and grass.

"A dog... a dog or something must have brought it here," she told herself, still scanning for any sign of threatening movement.

"Yeah, a dog." She closed the door again and walked back into the apartment, staring at Old Dog, who looked like he was dozing again.

She couldn't help but feel like she was trapped in her apartment, and that something was waiting. Curled around her apartment like a cat waiting at a mouse-hole.

LETTING GO

That night, Old Dog died.

"No, no, no, no!" Katy was curled up with his heavy head in her lap, her tears dripping into his fur where they beaded up and rolled down his cheeks before absorbing into his brittle coat. "Please, please, don't leave me." Katy rocked back and forth, bumping her head against the wall.

"I don't want you to say goodbye, not yet. I'm not ready to go," Katy moaned, sipping small bits of breath between her torrent of tears. The sadness felt like it was going to crack open her ribcage.

"Please."

The day has started as many had, with her scrounging around in a grocery store about thirty minutes away from home. The one closest to her had been infested with rather territorial raccoons. Old Dog had stayed home. No amount of luring him with bits of stale crackers and even some canned meat had been able to get him to climb from the bed in the corner. Katy had been on the hunt for more bottled water for her and Old Dog, and canned wet food for him. The last of his teeth seemed to do him no good for kibble anymore, and she was desperate to get him to eat. His ribs had begun poking out of his rough fur, which had lost any shine and fell out in big clumps when she petted him.

The room felt so quiet without his dog-noises—a quiet that felt maddening. The silence roared against her ears as she held him. She had come in the front door and her heart had dropped when he hadn't come trotting up to her, his usual happy grin on his worn face. That had been when she'd found him, lying down facing the wall. When she'd dove to his side, he had given her one weak thump of his tail, one more look up into her dark eyes with his own dark eyes. One last wheezing breath out, and he hadn't breathed in again.

He died with a peaceful smile on his face.

Katy let out a loud wail, followed by soft punctuations of hiccups and moans. Her trembling hand stroked his soft floppy ears.

"I know... hic... I know you were ready... but I'm not." Katy's voice sounded far away as she talked to Old Dog's quiet shape, like she was talking to him down the long hallway of her throat. He had only been with her for a few months, but she had loved him fiercely. This felt worse than any breakup with a partner.

Katy pulled the blanket over him after cupping his cheek and giving his ratty ears one last tug. Sobbing, she curled up on the couch with her hand still resting on his cooling body. The quiet around her felt like she was drowning in the dark as she said goodbye to her only friend.

In the morning, she dug a hole in the backyard. She was glad that they had made it through the Winter and the ground wasn't frosted, though in the Spring air, there was still a bite of coolness. She dug and dug, deeper than she probably needed to go. Then, she stood there in the cool morning air, letting the sunrise glare into her tear-stained eyes for what felt like hours.

Finally, she went inside and stared at the blanket that covered her only friend in this new, lonely world. With some effort, she scooped him up and carried him outside. She gently laid his body in the ground and then covered the hole up and sat on the dry, dead grass, staring at the raw earth. Letting her fists gather handfuls of muddy ground and let them go. She looked at her run-down apartment. Home for the last three years.

Her skin prickled, and she looked behind her. For a moment, she could have sworn she'd seen something. A smudge in the corner of her eye, the feeling like something was watching her. Her heart jumped in her chest, and she let go of the handful of dirt she had been squeezing.

"Hello?" she called out.

Every once in a while, she would still try to call for people. Hoping that someone would walk out from the other side of the house and give her a big old "hello" greeting. She had spent so much time, back when the world had been normal, trying to ignore and avoid other people. Now, she got it.

It didn't feel like there was much point to being alive if you were the only one left.

"So, what do I do, as the last dumb human on Earth? I can't reproduce; we can't continue the species. We're extinct… I'm just still kicking for a little while," she said, talking down to the mound of earth where Old Dog lay.

"What do you think, Old Dog? Your owners left you alone outside all the time. Was life still worth living?" He didn't reply.

She threw down the shovel and went inside to start packing her things.

The loss was bitter and would come over her in waves as she tried to hold back a waterfall of tears. The two of them had seen plenty of other loose dogs during their adventures around the Bay Area, but those other dogs weren't Old Dog.

"It's time to go," she said to herself. "It's time to move on. I can't do anything else here." She slammed the door and paced around her apartment. Maybe there were people somewhere else? She had given up too easily. The world was calling her to discover its secrets. To unwind what had happened. At the very least, to see it before she breathed her last breath. And she didn't have any reason to continue living in this ground-level apartment where she would always be listening for a dog's soft footfalls.

Katy usually loved this time of year, when life bloomed again. Right now, though, she wasn't thinking at all about the first life of Spring. She could only think about how badly she wanted to get away from this apartment, and how much it hurt to lose Old Dog. The pristine lawns of her neighbors that had gone a gray-brown during the Winter were growing wildly, and not just with grass. Small trees were bursting through the seams of sidewalks, pushing away the unnatural blocks of stone. The air roared with the early activity of insects in the warmer air. More had changed than just people being gone… a wildness was creeping into the world.

She didn't pack much, only some clothes and food. The items that she'd used to prize didn't matter as much anymore. The clothes went in a hamper in the back of the car, and the rest of the space was for cases and cases of water. The apartment still looked lived in as she stared across it at the doorway one last time. The empty bed frame, the couch with sheets and bedding thrown over it. Dirty dishes still in the sink. Taking one last look at the painting she loved, she walked out, leaving the front door wide open.

Let the wild take it all.

On the way out of town, she saw a sporting goods store off to the right. Pulling off of the highway, she drove up to the entrance and pried open the automatic doors. The mannequin posing in the entryway startled her for a moment. People! A leap of excitement in her heart fizzled out when she saw its white, expressionless face. Katy looked behind her, waiting for Old Dog to trot into the empty store to begin his usual patrol. Her face fell when she remembered where she had left him.

The store looked like it could be opening in a few hours, nothing out of place. The shelves were stacked with expensive hiking backpacks and techy gear for camping geeks. Now, they were a lifeline. The water-safe tablets, cooking stove, climbing gear. All of it was gold, and it was hers for the taking. In this way, she was grateful that she didn't have anyone else to compete with for the last stuff in the world.

Katy browsed the aisles. She would stop to strip down to try on a pair of tough hiking pants or new shoes. If it fit and she didn't already have something like it with her, it went into a cart that she'd taken from the front. She scooped every one of the dehydrated hiking meals off of the shelves—even the flavors she knew she wouldn't like. They didn't take up much space, and she didn't know if where she was going would have an REI. She was grateful that her parents had loved to camp when she'd been growing up. Thinking of them gave her a pang of guilt that she hadn't raced up to Portland yet, but she knew what was waiting for her there. When the cart began to get full of the food goods and clothes, she rolled it out to the car and carefully packed the back before going back into the store again. What would she need? She wasn't camping anymore; she would need to survive. Opening a book from the front about outdoor survival, she used it as a checklist to verify she had everything she'd need. Cooking fuel? Check. Extra water bottles? Check. First-aid gear… well, the store didn't have much beyond the basics, but it would work for now.

She hurried past the pet-goods section with her cart full again, feeling her eyes well with tears as she looked at the aisle. Out of habit mostly, she walked past the cash registers on her final way out. Taking a granola bar from the bin near the register and dumping the rest of the bin into the cart, she then munched on her snack as she walked out of the store.

She gave the mannequin that had scared her at the entrance a salute and was off. *Goodbye, Berkeley.* She had a feeling she would never come back—there wasn't anything for her here. She'd left most of her research in a neat pile on the kitchen table, thesis abandoned.

None of that mattered.

PRISTINE

Despite the aching question that she still didn't want answered about home, about Portland, she didn't drive there. The Spring was waking up the world and she wanted to go where it was wildest after spending Winter in a city that was a tomb of humanity. Before *it* had happened, she'd usually gone camping for at least a week every year. Sometimes completely by herself, like she was going to do now. Sometimes with a few college friends or her mom and dad. Danielle had hated camping, so she'd never come with her. But it had always been a time for Katy to reset and refocus on what she wanted next. Just her and the night sky and early cold mornings making breakfast over a camp stove or a fire. She needed to run away from the heartbreak of losing her only friend in this new world.

As she drove, tears freely leaked down her cheeks, and she rubbed the steering wheel with her thumbs until it was warm in places. Just trying to do something with her body to keep the sorrow from seeping in and taking hold. She played with the air vents, and a gold dog hair drifted through the car across her face.

Katy had been on the road for two hours now and had one hour to go until she would reach the entrance of Yosemite. Her eyes felt tired, so she pulled off to find somewhere to stretch her legs and take a break. Driving through the quiet streets, she looked for a good place to stop. The neighborhood she passed through looked unkempt, but still like people could be living there. She felt sure that the wear and tear on buildings would start to show soon, now that no one was there to repaint after the colder months; there'd be no patches in the roads that had been damaged as ice and snow had frozen and melted, and frozen and melted again, ripping holes into the asphalt. Since there was no epic disaster to damage buildings, no nuclear bomb, it would take much longer before the world of man started to look abandoned. She almost wished it could be destroyed, so that it would feel less like she was a ghost wandering through the pristine streets alone.

Something told her to stop, and she pumped the brake pedal hard. She'd been driving through a cookie-cutter neighborhood with townhomes and some stand-alone houses. The kind of neighborhood someone would want to live in with their boring spouse to raise kids. She bet the school district had been great here. She pulled over the car, a strange feeling coming over her. Something was wrong—very wrong. It was a similar wrongness to when JD had sat up in her bed months ago and begun to scream. The same desperation filled the air here. She got out of the car, walking toward the feeling. Following it like an animal on a scent trail, bullet-straight. Even though every nerve in her body told her to stop, to turn and run in bounding leaps. Run, rabbit, run.

Nothing looked sinister in the warm mid-afternoon sun. She had stopped in front of a set of townhouses with small trim gardens in the front, all of the plants now overgrown and bursting through the wooden fences that separated each unit. There, in the window of the unit to the far-right... She could have sworn she'd seen something move, and the light-tan curtains that framed the front window shift. The windowsill had a small stone stag figurine on the inside, and a row of candles.

She walked, almost in a trance, toward the townhouse. Her hand grabbed the doorknob and she paused there, body pressed close to the door. The metal was cold in her warm hand as she turned the knob, and the door opened easily, unlocked.

"Hello?" she called, hoping and also very much not hoping that there would be a reply.

As usual, there was no reply, and she walked out of the entryway. Whoever had lived there had been one of those precise, neat minimalists who scowled at children. The carpet was perfectly white, with no signs of stains. The chairs at the glass dining table were all tucked in precisely the right way. Even the books on the bookshelf in the corner were in alphabetical order. Katy felt a little guilty about not taking her shoes off while imagining the owner of this home. Her boots echoed through the entryway, and she avoided looking at herself in the mirror placed below the coat rack.

She swore she heard a small sound from farther into the townhome, and she followed it on tiptoe through the dining room toward the kitchen. And as she came around the corner into the kitchen, she gasped. The kitchen, with its white cabinets and white center island with soft gray granite countertops, was completely covered in blood. She gripped the sides of the hallway in horror as her eyes raced over the scene in front of her. *Red*. It was all red. Not the old red-brown color of dried blood, but a raw, new crimson on the white porcelain tiles of the floor. The splashes of blood started halfway down the kitchen island, covering the floor in thick pools toward the back door. Bloody handprints gripped the handle of the fridge, which was now hanging ajar. The handprints then covered the edge of the island and then appeared on the floor. She thought she could see a few fingernails and claw marks on the tiles. It looked like someone had been dragged from the house against their will while every pore of their body had been bleeding. There were even splatters on the ceiling. One section of the ceiling that was particularly wet went *drip, drip, drip* onto the kitchen island below. The dripping was the only sound, and now she knew that was what she'd heard from the living room. The metallic smell of blood stung her nostrils.

Katy's heart played a metal anthem in her chest, screaming at her to get away from this red room. The blood must have been fresh, it was so bright red. She stepped onto it, and it made the sticky bar-room sound. Maybe a little older than she'd expected. She treaded carefully through the mess—she had to get to that back door. What was behind that door? Could it have been the second-to-the-last person on Earth? What had happened to them that could cause something like this?

"It's just red, Katy, it's just red." Her hand was trembling as she reached the door handle. Her fingers slipped off the first time, coming away sticky and wet. She regripped more firmly and flung open the door.

The back patio stared back at her, tidy and gray. She craned her neck out and looked around. Stepping down onto the stairs, her feet made small sticky sounds, but the stairs had been clean before her feet marked them. She closed the door and looked at the backyard, which was clean. She opened the door and looked at the mess again. Still there. She did this several more times, trying to put together how someone could have made it through that door bleeding that much and have not let a single drop of blood fall once they'd left the townhouse.

The feeling she had was *wrong, wrong, wrong*, and then gone as soon as she stepped out of the kitchen. She gaped at the kitchen from the outside, pulling at her cheeks and the ends of her hair. Someone had been ripped from this world, and they'd gone out fighting. She imagined the tight-lipped, high-bunned middle-aged woman who'd probably lived here alone. With her tidy white kitchen, who in the middle of the night had felt that same *wrong, wrong, wrong* feeling. The force that had sucked every person out of this world had had other plans for the line-mouthed schoolteacher.

Katy plopped down onto the back steps, cradling her head in her hands. Her hair stuck out at odd angles from her loose ponytail. Desperately, she wanted to think of something she could do here other than stare, an uninvited onlooker to some terrible crime. She couldn't help but think of her nightmares, where she was hunted. And the glimpses out of the corner of her eye, suggesting that something might be following her. And the dead squirrel at her doorstep. Probably left by a dog or a cat, but maybe not.

That kitchen would become one of her regular nightmares for the rest of her life.

Pulling herself from her fretting, she willed herself to get up. Brushing the back of her pants off, she went back to the car, around through the side yard instead of walking through the house again. She missed Old Dog, his head resting near the shifter and looking up at her with his clouded eyes. The car hummed back to life, and she headed down the empty roads. She would drive carefully and slowly as night approached. More animals were likely to wander into the road now that most of the traffic was gone.

She had to stop several times as a deer or a cow stared at her from the middle of the road. Her hands didn't stop shaking for what felt like hours after that red room in the white house.

THE CAPTAIN

She pulled into the parking lot of the visitor center for Yosemite National Park. In the dark, her headlights illuminated the spiraling dust. The parking lot was completely empty, framing the low stone building. The night was overcast, so the forest around her was dark, but Katy knew that beyond the parking lot and the trees framing it was the crest of stony peaks and mountains. The air was cold as she stepped out of the car, her breath coming out in hot puffs as she took a crowbar from the back seat. The glass of the visitor center door cracked slightly when she pried the door loose, but it didn't shatter to pieces.

She unloaded the gas tanks, her food, and her sleeping mat, and tossed it all onto the floor in the main room of the visitor center, next to a rack of maps and brochures. Once she had finished unloading the car, she made a makeshift bed behind the front desks, tucked between two filing cabinets. A taxidermied deer kept her company, and the exhibits around her showing maps of the park lulled her to sleep.

She woke up when the sun started streaming through the dusty windows. Without electricity to keep the lights on, she'd begun sleeping when the sun went down and waking when it came up again. Having never really been a morning person before (hell, she'd been nocturnal before during her work in Austin), the change of pace felt refreshing. Today, she laid on the floor for some time while she examined every crack in the well-worn hardwood floor and the scuffs and scratches on the tan-painted walls. She had a tendency to lose herself in the details now. She would stay frozen in one place while her mind explored the world around her and made inner dialogues to keep her company. After about thirty minutes, her bladder demanded she get out of her warm sleeping bag. She stretched and opened the front door.

After strolling around the back of the building to relieve herself, she set up a small kitchen station. Breathing in the clean, crisp mountain air, she heated a can of beans on the small burner she had packed with her. As she waited for them to warm, she undid her hair and began to braid it into one long, neat pleat. She tied off the end, and it brushed her hips as she flipped it over her shoulder to give the beans another stir. After the first few months of panic and despair, and a good long conditioning with bottled water as a rinse, she had managed to work out most of the tangles. Now, she carefully brushed out and braided her hair for practical keeping. A few times, she had considered cutting it all off, but as soon as she went to get the scissors, she couldn't stomach the idea. Her hair had been long her entire life.

She remembered the last time she'd been at Yosemite. It had been crawling with sightseers from all over the world. Only a few people a year had gotten to hike the back-country area here, and they'd had to apply to a lottery for permits. Certain parks and trails had set a limit to the amount of people who could visit every year; the only way to get the permit had been to submit your information into the lottery. When Katy had arrived, amid the milling people at the entrance of the visitor center had been a harried-looking park ranger. Katy had pulled him aside to show him her ticket, and he'd scratched his head underneath his hat and told her that the park had had to be closed down that day due to a small fire that they were still trying to control. Someone had smoked a cigarette and thrown the still-burning butt into the dry brush.

She'd never gotten to hike after she had won that lottery, and now was her chance. She remembered how disappointed she'd been, with her car full of gear and the whole weekend to hike and hike hard. On the way back to Berkeley, she had cried out of frustration for most of the drive. But the whole park was hers now. No park ranger could tell her that there was a fire warning and she couldn't hike. She was free.

The sun was already warming up the cool Spring morning air as she sat on the steps of the visitor center, eating her breakfast out of a camping mug. A squirrel chittered at her and scrambled up a nearby tree, spinning around in a spiral as it climbed. It would pause every few feet and peek around the tree at her, flicking its fluffy tail while its small body stayed frozen. Katy smiled, watching the sassy behavior. The squirrel was warning her to stay away from its babies and communicating that she wasn't welcome up in the trees. Katy wasn't going to chase the squirrel, though. The squirrel seemed pleased with the warning and settled up higher in the branches, still keeping a wary eye on the predator below her.

The world was going on as it always had.

It was typical of humanity to assume that the world would crumble when humanity crumbled. That the end of humanity would be the end of this planet. *We wouldn't like to think about how everything continued on without us.* Any story of the end of the world came with ruin to everything around it, as though humanity had built it all, so it all must come crumbling down just the same. Katy kicked a stone, which rattled across the ground and elicited another shower of curses from the red squirrel high up in the tree.

This earth had been here long before humanity. Humanity was a relatively new scar on Earth's surface and had existed on her own for more time than she had with people. The dinosaurs had also thought (if they'd been smart enough, which they probably hadn't) that, when they ended, so would all life on Earth. It had not. Earth had made room for something new—many new things, in fact. Katy thought about the impact of humans on this earth, which was probably equal to a meteor in the end. Earth would have survived the meteor, so it would probably survive this. Even if all of the nuclear plants melted down (she had been trying to avoid thinking about them), and all life was wiped out, the planet would likely keep spinning on. Maybe life wouldn't come back except for tiny bacteria for some time afterward, but it would come back. There were special bacteria that lived on volcanic vents in the ocean, and they would probably survive a nuclear winter. Katy wouldn't, though.

Though that thought kept repeating itself in her mind, gnawing away at her comfort and sanity, at this moment, with the warm morning sun shining on her as she watched a squirrel spiral up the tree, it was a comfort. All of this would be okay without her. She felt slightly hopeful when she thought about this bigger picture. She had spent her life studying the natural world, and she loved it. It comforted her that its beauty would remain long after she herself began fertilizing the ground.

She let her meal settle in her stomach while she watched the trees wave back and forth. When the sun grew warm enough to make her skin tingle, she packed up her items in the visitor center. Katy wanted to go on a hike. Perhaps a strange choice after discovering how alone she was, but for her, hikes offered the environment where her thoughts were the most tamed. Where she could lose herself in the rhythm of her boots on a trail, winding between the dust and the jutting rocks and roots. The call of the trails demanded that she see the raw, untamed world. The reminders of her loss were far behind her, for now. She had spent an entire Winter hiding in a shabby apartment in Berkeley, California, trying to lie to herself about reality. It was time to do whatever she wanted. And, right now, she wanted to hike this mountain. Then, afterward, she could think about things and places that she would rather not consider right now. Like home, and her family.

About thirty minutes later, she had filled her hiking pack, carefully weighted with her camping gear and all of the backpacking items she would need for the long trail in front of her. She packed everything she wouldn't need into the car and walked toward the weathered sign for the trailhead. Off she went.

The walking calmed her mind, and the worry about nuclear winters and what had happened to her family slipped from her thoughts. She let the burn in her thighs and calves fuel her forward, as she had let it do many times before. Katy loved the national parks. When someone asked her what her favorite thing was about America, the parks were always her answer. They held so much raw, untamed variety. Although the most recent government had tried, they hadn't managed to dismantle the entire national parks system. Some parks that held important natural resources had been stripped, but so far, Yosemite had been a popular enough destination that the people had pushed back. Now, the parks were a little bit wilder.

Strangely enough, being where she was helped her pretend like the world was normal outside of the park. She very well could be hiking the trail just like she'd been planning to hike it last year. In the city, people were just waking up to their weekends, to start spending time with their families and washing their cars. She smiled at the thought, imagining someone else coming down the path and waving with the typical hiker's hello.

No one passed her and waved. A light breeze stirred the trees, but they were the only things waving to her as she passed.

It was mid-day before she stopped to snack on the side of the trail. She pulled out a planner notebook and marked off the date—still trying to keep track of time. Her chewing paused as she saw the note she had written about today; it was her father's birthday.

She thought about Tom Johnson, "Dad" for her whole life. He didn't look anything like her, with freckled white skin and crinkled, happy blue eyes. He would always laugh and tell her that love was what family was, not appearances. She thought about his last birthday, when she had flown up to Portland as a surprise. She'd brought a stack of books from the used bookstore down the street from her home. He read more than anyone she knew when he wasn't working at an accounting firm in downtown Portland. A simple guy, really. Who had really wanted to have kids, and when her mom hadn't been able to get pregnant, they'd gotten Katy. An angry bundle all the way from China, who'd cried all day and all night for the first few weeks they had her. That angry bundle had grown into a girl who stared under rocks at all the bugs and brought home dead birds with the enthusiasm of a proud kitten. Katy was lucky, she knew, to have been raised by a family that loved her so much and loved each other. She ached, thinking about the quiet weekends where the three of them would have breakfast together and play with the dogs.

She wiped away hot tears from her cheek. For a moment, she could almost feel Dad's hand, warm and heavy on her shoulder, as she sat there.

"Hey, little Kitty Kat," he would say, brushing her long black hair away from her face as she scribbled furiously, her tongue pinched halfway out through her lips. "How 'bout you take a break and come on a walk with me?"

"Yeah, of course, Dad," Katy said out loud, to the memory. She took a swig from her water bottle and held it up to the sky, a final cheers.

"Let's go for a walk."

She hiked until her feet throbbed and she could feel wetness in her socks, which she suspected was her toes being rubbed raw by her new hiking boots. The sun was starting to set along the pine-lined horizon, and her shoulders ached from the heavy pack. Katy spied a perfect spot on the trail, overlooking an expansive canyon with a flat area for her tent. The tent went up quickly, and she barely fumbled with the poles. Once she was finished, she pulled the sleeping mat partway out of the mouth of the tent and plopped down. One boot came off and then the other. She cringed as her socks stuck to her feet as she pulled. They came away, and she saw that her toes were red and angry, with crusted blood around most of the toenails. She sighed and gave her toes a weak wiggle. New hiking boots were always a bitch. It would have been smarter to wear the old pair instead of the new pair she'd taken from the store.

That Winter, she hadn't done much of anything except for sleep, cry, and walk with Old Dog. The pain felt good, though; it felt real. It was one of the first things that didn't feel like a bad dream in a long time. Each of her toes glowed like hot coal was being pressed to it now that the pressure from walking had been relieved. She stuck her feet away from her sleeping pad and poured a small amount of water on her toes, wiggling them back and forth against the stream of water. It stung, but the cold water also felt good after their being cramped in the boots all day. Conscious of how much water she had, she only gave her toes a short rinse and then took a swig of the water.

Soon after, sleep came heavy and hard. She slipped into deep and earthy dreams that would be lit up by little sparks of awakening as she listened to the night sounds of the forest. And then something edged into her sleep-mind. Something that made her sit upright.

It was still night, but the moon was large and the sky bright with stars, so she could see well in a black, white, and blue hue. Twigs were snapping outside of the tent, and it sounded like footsteps. Katy scrambled to her knees and unzipped the tent as quietly as she could. Her body screamed in protest over her movements, already sore and stiff from the hard hike. Her toes stung as she shifted her weight onto her bare feet and peered out of the tent. *There*. Something moved. Something vaguely human-shaped, that was just around the corner of the trail. With not a moment to waste, she scrambled after it, wearing only her loose hiking pants. She had taken off her shirt and bra when she'd begun to sweat in the sleeping bag. Half-naked, she crawled up the trail, touching her hands to the ground in order to stay in a low crouch. The shape was always just out of full view, curving around a corner or leaping off of the path. One moment, she was sure it was a person full and upright, wearing a long coat. The next moment, she wasn't sure if it was a thing at all. Maybe it was a patch of smoke in the corner of her vision, like the one she had seen when she'd buried Old Dog or when the power had gone out for the first time. The visions like this had come more and more as her time alone had stretched longer. This was the first time she'd kept seeing a shape, though, and not just in the corner of her eye. But what if it was a person? Another person! She needed to know.

She didn't pay attention to how far she was running from the camp with no flashlight or gear. The moon was bright enough that she could see with her dark-adjusted eyes. The only thing in her mind was that shape. She had to catch up to it, even as new cuts bloomed on her bare feet and the branches of trees whipped at her arms and torso. Before she knew it, she was above the path on a steep incline. Just ahead of her, above a patch of rocks, was the edge of the thing's long black cloak. Determined to get there before the shape moved away again, she prepared to scramble up the rocks. She gripped the out-cropping firmly and, with a grunt, swung herself up in a big leap onto the flat surface above her.

And landed face to face with a big fat black bear.

"Oh!"

The bear's nose was almost close to touching her own.

The bear shied away, the whites of her eyes showing. She stood up on her hind feet, huge clawed paws hanging down near her stomach. Towering over Katy. Katy glanced back at the direction she'd come from. Going down would be much harder than getting up had been. The bear let out an angry huff, and then the paws crashed down in a rounded-back bear dance. Bears would do this as a threat, and Katy knew the warning well. Katy reeled backward, her arms flailing for a grip behind her and finding only air. The bear grunted, and Katy yelped as she fell. Trees and branches clawed at her, breaking her fall. Her head bounced off of a rock, hard. The whole time, her arms flailed wildly and she saw glimpses of the bear still standing above her. She landed in an explosion of broken branches. A pain sharper than any pain she had ever felt before blinded her vision. She clutched her thigh as she took big fish-out-of-water gulps of the air and red spots danced back and forth across her eyes. And then her vision came back long enough for her to stare at the origin of her agonizing pain. Her thigh was a wet mess of blood, and she thought she could see something poking out of her leg just to the right of the bone.

In the blackness, as her consciousness began to slip from her, she thought to herself, *The last human on Earth. I'm the last person on Earth, and I'm going to die in the forest impaled by a tree because I got scared by a big fat black bear. I've got to stop running into things and falling backward... what an idiot.* Everything felt wet, with what she assumed was her own blood. She gripped her thigh tight around the branch and cried out. *Black bears aren't even aggressive. That bear was probably just as scared of me.*

She let go, into complete blackness.

CHEW AND PULL

She awoke, the gnawing pain in her whole body demanding attention. The pain had chewed away at her blackout sleep until the whole world was screaming at her. The sick hot sun was blasting down on her through the canopy of fragrant pine trees. Her breath felt like she was squeezing it out of a pair of rusted bellows, creaking and painful. But the pain. Oh, the pain. Her feet were uphill, and her head felt like a hot air balloon because she had been lying there with all of her blood rushing to it. Her head was nestled in between clumps of scrub oak brush.

"Oh God." She closed her eyes, looking at the blind, red through-the-eyelids world.

She couldn't decide if she was pleasantly surprised that she was still alive or wished that she wasn't. Because she was alone in the forest, and even if she walked out of the forest, there would be no one to hold her close and sew up her wounds. There would be no birthday party for her dad, and she wouldn't teach the incoming freshman about general biology. She would never meet a special someone to share her life with… and, hell, she wouldn't even get to sit in the back of a dark movie theater with her smuggled-in candies and watch a new film.

She would also probably never walk normally again, if the wound in her leg was as bad as she imagined it to be.

Finally, she willed her eyes to open. The sickening sun stabbed her unprepared eyes. She looked at her leg and almost passed out from the pain of moving her head. What she had originally imagined as her bone jutting out from her thigh or a massive branch penetrating her leg wasn't quite as bad as all that. Still, a broken branch had managed to rip her hiking pants and stab a good distance into the outer area of her middle thigh, mostly through what she guessed were superficial skin layers. It was jutting out of her thigh. Her pants were covered in blood all the way up to her crotch. Some of the blood was already rust-brown and dried. She guessed that her landing with her head down meant that her blood had rushed to her head instead of to her leg. *Stupid. Lucky.* She guessed that if the wound had been any closer toward her inner thigh, she would have bled out in seconds in an artery-spurt, panicked death. Her leg wasn't twisted at a strange angle. How she hadn't bled to death was a miracle. A miracle that she worried would end as soon as she moved around.

Based on her sickly, pounding headache, waves of nausea, and the weakness she felt all over, she had lost a good amount of blood. Moaning, she bit her lip and tried to wiggle the toes of her right leg, which had the nasty wound. Though her toes were covered in dirt and tinged slightly blue, they wiggled when her mind commanded it. The wiggling did send more stabs of pain all the way from her ankle up into her groin, but at least her leg worked. The branch was a jagged point—created from a snapped branch, she guessed. It was sticky and covered in her blood and dirt.

She rolled her head to the side and looked up the hill to where she had fallen from. It had been quite a tumble. As she tried to dry-swallow through the golf ball in her throat, she looked over her body again. Her stomach, chest, and even one of her nipples had angry red scrapes and deep cuts. From protecting herself during the fall, her arms were covered in scratches. Her chest heaved up and down, and she felt tired. No, she couldn't sleep now. She thought about the med kit that was probably only a few hundred feet away at her camp. Maybe she could salvage this. She tried to remember what she was supposed to do now. She knew precious little about how to take care of injured humans. During her undergraduate studies, she had taken some veterinary science courses, and she prayed that most of the knowledge she retained from those lessons applied to people, as well.

Ignoring the sickly waves of nausea and pain that trembled through her body when she moved, she reached underneath herself to see if the stick that was stabbing through her leg was attached to anything bigger. She found that it seemed to have been attached to a downed tree, but her fall onto the stick had luckily loosened the branch from the rotted trunk. A few wiggles of the stick (which each made her let out a blood-curdling scream that echoed against the shale and dirt hillside), and it was free. She rolled forward onto her already scraped palms.

The pain would crash over her like a wave that left her panting for breath, and just as she took in a few deep breaths, it would crash on her again. She threw up in the moist dirt at the base of a pine tree. Staring at the pile of her own sick as it soaked into the dirt, she willed herself to move.

"Come on, move, move." Her encouraging words to herself came out as croaks. Fingernails digging into the soil, she started to move again.

Crawling down the hiking trail that was deteriorated and damaged from the Winter snows, she moved down toward her camp with her belly scraping and dragging along the rough trail. She wasn't sure if she was able to stand up yet. She felt so weak, it felt safer to crawl. Around this time of year, the rangers would normally have come and patched up the trail, building up areas where Winter erosion had worn it away. Not this year. *My camp is just around the corner*, she thought to herself. *I can get there and have a drink of water.* Her tongue felt like a dead, dried-up lizard in her mouth, scaly and clawed.

"Fuck, fuck, fuck, fuck. Oh, fuck…." She had come around the corner and her tent wasn't there. While chasing the stupid, fat bear, she must have gone even farther than she'd thought in her desperation.

She collapsed into the dirt, and the world went black again. A curious coyote strolled by, edging around her body, sniffing the small trail of blood behind her before jumping away when Katy groaned. The coyote was gone by the time Katy's eyes opened again, unaware that she had almost become dinner.

Ugh, I'm still alive. She was dismayed and hopeful, given the fact that she hadn't slipped into a forever darkness. Despite the suffering and loneliness that she had experienced over the last few months, she didn't want to die yet. Biting down on her tongue, she tested her ability to stand up. She managed a crouch and used a big stone on the edge of the trail to haul herself to her feet. The injured leg gave out, but if she used rocks and the steep side of the trail to cling to as she stumbled forward, she was able to walk. Her hands looked pale every time they reached out in front of her. From fingertips to elbows, her arms were covered in an angry tangle of cuts and scrapes. Coming around the corner, she saw her tent sitting untouched. A few more heaving crawls later, she was able to reach into the tent and paw around for her water bottle.

The water hurt as she gulped it down. She hauled herself into a sitting position in front of the tent and examined her leg and the rest of her body as best she could. Her hands explored the pains of her body. Really, it didn't feel like she had a single spot that didn't hurt, but there were some cuts that were deeper than others. It felt like the gash in her head could do with some stitches, but she wasn't sure how she was going to do that. What really mattered, though, was the stick that was still jutting out of her right leg, like an ugly arm waving at her and saying, *Hey! Hey! You're going to die!* She bit her lip so hard that it started to bleed as she examined the stick more closely. It was like a gruesome piercing on the outside of her thigh. She tried to guess how deep it was with her fingertips and moved them away when fresh dribbles of blood seeped out of the wound. She knew she desperately needed that blood.

With weak, trembling hands, she fumbled with the med kit. Items flew out as her shaking hands pawed through it. Her eyelids felt heavy. With the gauze pressed close to the leg wound, she examined it again, timidly. She was about to gently pull on the stick when a nagging thought in the back of her head told her, *Better not.* With her pocketknife, she instead tested sawing the extra bit off. If she worked very, very carefully and held it steady next to the wound, she was able to cut the stick slightly shorter. The task took her almost an hour, as she had to stop several times to cry and sip on water. *I'm still going to die,* she thought to herself. *Even if I somehow manage to hike all the way back down this goddamn mountain and get to my car, I'm going to die from an infection. Or I'll go into septic shock.*

Despite her inner monologue telling her that she was going to die, she kept doing things to keep herself living. The reason why escaped her, and she was somewhat amused about it. *The human condition, we want to live so desperately.* She leaned back, cleaning off the wounds she could reach, and poured a capful of hydrogen peroxide onto her scalp where the deep gash was still oozing blood.

It bubbled and fizzed, and the carbonated blood trickled down her temple. It felt like pop rocks on her skull, or ants climbing into the wound and rearranging their dirt mound. Her teeth chattered together in pain. She dug her fingers into the dirt, waiting for the fizzing to stop. Her eyes kept wandering to the stick. She remembered in TV shows and books that you weren't supposed to pull something like this out. Eventually, it would have to come out… but, for now, she thought she better not try it here.

The gauze ran out, but she managed to bandage up the worst gashes. She still had a stick poking out of her leg, but she tried not to think about it. Taking deep, hungry breaths, she leaned back against a rock. Her gaze wandered to Half-Dome, the impressive granite mountain that Yosemite was so famous for. The morning sun was glowing over it across the valley from her, kissing the bright blue sky that showed barely a cloud. The day was beautiful. The day was beautiful, and she was dying. A bird whizzed by, chirping loudly. A thin line of ants marched along the dusty path, each carrying a small piece of plant. The world was moving around her as she tried to breathe through the pain. As she sipped more water, she tried to memorize the image of how the waterfall roaring over the edge of the granite cliff-face looked. She tried to imagine the cool spray of the waterfall on her skin. If that was the last thing she saw, then damn, she was lucky.

Salt, sugar. She was hungry. A deep instinct in her pushed her to survive. With her weak left hand, she pulled her pack closer and leaned it up against a stone near the tent. She found a protein bar and fussed with the wrapper, letting her gaze fall back onto the mountains. Eating the bar felt like nothing; she didn't even taste it as she mechanically chewed and swallowed each bite.

Time passed in a blur as she lay there, trying to feed and water herself. Sunset began to bloom across the horizon. Katy was shocked to see it so soon. She willed herself to move again, pushing herself up from her crouched position. She crawled into the open tent. Every move was like swimming through molasses, heavy and slow. She couldn't see herself and she was glad of that, but if she could have, she would have thought she was a zombie. Covered in blood, practically naked, and wearing only the tattered remains of hiking pants. Using the last ounce of her energy, she tossed the sleeping bag over her, leaving her impaled leg poking out the unzipped side, and stared up at the stars through the tent's opening. At least she could see them one last time.

Her eyes opened in the morning light. *Alive, still.* Nothing truly smelled as sweet as the wind blowing through an empty pine forest. The leg wound was beginning to look red and angry around the edges. Every muscle in her body was in knots and bruised or torn. The strength was being sapped out of her, moment by moment. It was now or never.

She still felt wobbly and weak, but she had enough energy to pack up her essentials. She left the tent behind, as she had a feeling that if she lived through this, she could happily take a long break from camping. The coyote had come back that night, disappointed that his potential snack hadn't died yet. He'd left a clumpy, bug-filled poo near her, marking his potential meal. Very slowly, lacing her hiking boots onto her feet, she prepared to walk away from her catastrophic injury.

"Uuuuugh." Straining with every one of her damaged muscles, she heaved herself up. She looked at the blood smeared all over the campsite. How was she still alive? Maybe it looked worse than it was. Still, her weak, trembling hands and deathly pale skin told her otherwise.

"I need to get moving."

Luck seemed to be on her side, and she found a nice long stick with only a few small branches to lean on, and then she began her trek down the trail. Every hop was agony, and she thought about how boldly she had climbed up this very path the other day with a comfortable burn in her legs.

As the day bled on one limping step at a time, Katy started to recognize the beginning of the trail. She stopped around mid-day and managed a short nap against a pine tree. Now the end was in sight. *You're still going to die, though*, the voice in her head said. *You have a stick going through your leg, and you're the only person left on Earth.* She shook the nagging voice away. She had never felt so weak in her whole life. Tears stung her scraped cheeks, and she sobbed as she continued to drag one foot in front of the other down the hiking path. She sobbed about the injustice of it all. Why her? Why was she here, seemingly alone? What had she done to be punished like this?

Sometime later, the path widened out and she saw the visitor center. When she got to the car, she collapsed in relief, leaning against the passenger side door. Where she leaned left a clean patch on the metal, as the rest of the car was covered in thick yellow pollen. Pine pollen dusted everything. If Katy hadn't been actively dying, she probably would have been sneezing from the pollen and cursing her swollen eyes.

Dropping the stick to the ground, she began to move herself around the car to the back. With trembling fingers, she managed to open the hatch, ducking out of the way of the door. She sat and slid her backpack off, still weeping as she did it. The bag fell heavy over her stacks of water and cans of food. She drank deeply from bottled water. Every swallow stabbed like a knife on her raw and thirsty throat. Shaking, she undid the button of what was left of her pants, moving them partway down her hips and ripping the rest of the fabric away. She took her pocketknife from her bag and cut off her underwear.

Leaning heavily against the car, pressing her forehead into the pine-dust on the roof, she slid her legs open wide enough to pee without dirtying herself too much. She could feel the hot spray drench her shoes and trickle down her left leg, but it was the best she could do. How was she going to drive like this? Surely, she would crash after the first few minutes.

When she was done with her first pee in what felt like days, she closed up the back of her car and clawed her way to the driver's side.

At least a car crash would be a faster way to put me out of my misery, she thought to herself as she opened the door and lowered herself into the seat with a whimper. Naked except for hiking boots, she sat huddled in the seat and staring at the visitor center in front of her. First, she tried putting her right foot on the gas, pumping it with the engine still off. It hurt terribly, but she thought she could manage. To stop the maniacal shivering that was making her teeth rattle together, she pulled a blanket over her lap and found a sweatshirt she had thrown on the passenger seat. She left the leg with the stick poking out of the blankets. It felt hot and throbbing anyway, in contrast to the deep shiver the rest of her body felt.

"Okay, let's do this," her voice cracked. She didn't know exactly what she would do, but it was happening. She needed to get the stick out of her leg somehow—and she guessed that going somewhere with antibiotics and more medical supplies would be a good idea. The car started, and she slowly pulled out of the parking lot.

NOT READY YET

A fever was starting to bloom. Her skin felt red and hot, with small streaks of red dancing around the puncture wound in her thigh. The car was doing lazy swerves across the road as she entered a town. She had no idea what town it was.

Her eyes shut, and she startled awake when there was a shower of sparks and a loud scraping noise as her car edged into a concrete curb. She tried to sit more upright in the seat, scanning every sign for that holy grail—the H on a blue sign that would mean maybe, maybe, she would be able to haul herself into a creepy abandoned hospital and have more equipment to die on.

"Doesn't matter if you find a hospital, Katy, you're still going to lose more blood and probably die when you pull that stick out," she told herself, slamming the breaks with her left foot when she finally saw the hospital sign off to the right. "The only thing you've ever patched up are animals, and none of them ever had something straight through them."

She wiped a trickle of sweat from her brow. It left a track of clean skin on her dirt-smudged face.

A few minutes later, she shuddered when she saw the hospital. Dark, looming, brutalist, and empty. The sun was getting low in the sky behind the building. Pulling straight up to the sign that said "EMERGENCY" in bright red letters, she turned off the engine and dragged herself out of her car.

The fever was wrapping around her like a fire blanket while a bonfire raged beyond it. The heat thrummed at her ears and had her dripping in sweat. Panting, she stumbled to the side of the car. For a moment, her legs buckled inward so that she bashed her knee into the side of the car. With a grunt, she managed to pull herself up again, trying to ignore the sudden cold flash following her fire-hot sweating, itself causing her to shiver and tremble. She fumbled around at the back of the car, her hand slipping off the back handle several times before she managed to open it. The backpack felt like it weighed hundreds of pounds as she pulled it onto her shoulder and took out the flashlight. Her senses were dulled, and her vision pulsated with her heartbeat as she walked through the wide-open, automatic doors to the ER. When the electricity had failed, they must have popped open. Dust, evidence of animals, and abandoned equipment lined the halls. It was dark, the weak light of the setting sun barely filtering through the dust-covered windows.

The first room she looked into had a big crusted brown stain that was most certainly blood on the hospital bed. The red spots had become brown spots now. Her lurching limp echoed through the empty hallways, *thump, thump, thump*. The next room she opened was a supply closet.

Using the headlamp, which she'd pulled out of her pack to read through the bottles, she threw painkillers and antibiotics into her backpack and dragged the bag along behind her, no longer able to shoulder the weight.

I for sure look like a zombie, she thought to herself as she found a clean, empty hospital bed in a small room in the ER and hauled herself onto it. *At least there aren't zombies.* Although, if there had been zombies, she would have known what to be scared of, instead of constantly waiting for some invisible force to rip all of the bones out of her body and leave her as a smear in a perfectly white kitchen.

She took the first dose of antibiotics and some painkillers with the last swig of her bottled water, and then she yanked the rolling med kit closer to her. She didn't know what half the things on it were for, but she would try her best. Maybe she could get through this.

"Alright," she said to herself. She began to peel away the wrapping around her leg wound. A sick wet smell filled the air, and she fought with her gag reflex for a moment, swallowing hard over and over again. Saliva filled her mouth, willing her to empty the contents of her stomach. That smell was coming from *her*.

"I am so fucked," she said to herself.

She examined the wound. Then, she grabbed coagulating powder, thanking herself that she knew what it was, and began to gently tug the stick backward, out the way it had gone in. Every inch the stick slid, her vision bloomed with fireworks of pain, her breathing heaving up higher and higher. Tears and sweat trickled down her face. Fresh blood and pus oozed from the puncture, but it didn't begin to bleed heavily.

She let the stick clatter to the floor and looked down at what looked to her like at least a six-inch-long stick. Her visual measuring was interrupted as the world swam around her. Darkness took her as she lay limp in the cold, dark room.

She woke up soaked in sweat, the bed underneath her wet. Her hair was plastered to her forehead, and she was shivering. Everything was bathed in dim blue light from the full moon outside the windows of the hospital. Deep in a fever and groaning, she looked down at her leg. It looked bad, fat and swollen, but the red stain on the bed hadn't grown much. She realized how lucky she was that it hadn't bled heavily after she'd passed out. Still, the world was spinning as she lifted her head to examine her injury, so she let herself fall back onto the pillow. It was cold in the hospital, or maybe she was hot? It was always so hard to tell when you were sick with a fever.

She reached out for water... something. Her hands swiping wildly at the rolling table next to her, scissors and other tools clattered off of the stainless-steel tray and onto the hard linoleum floor.

She swung her legs—carefully, very carefully—to the side of the bed. Every movement felt like she was wrestling through tar. She tried to stand, using the bed as support. Instead, she collapsed to the floor, the pain in her leg searing. Through the fog of pain and fever, she felt something coming; it was just around the corner in the hallway. It was that *wrong, wrong, wrong* feeling. She could hear it crawling through the hall toward her.

A slithering scrape across the dust-covered tiles. Coming closer and closer.

"No, no, no, no, GO AWAY!" She waved wildly at the air in front of her, as though trying to shoo away a cloud of smoke with her fingers arched into claws. Trying to fight off the invisible fear that was trying to reach into her. On her hands and knees, she tried to crawl behind the bed to hide, doing so just as she saw a shadow darken the weak light coming from the hallway. She couldn't look away from the dim corridor.

Then it came, a black cloud of roiling smoke ripping around the corner. She was so scared that she couldn't even begin to make out what it was. It moved like a buzzing cloud of locusts, or a sentient smoke burning off of a poisonous oil field. It dove forward and filled her lungs, choking her mouth full of it, filling her tongue with the taste of burned meat and charcoal. The smoke surrounded her, clawing at her fever-torn body. Invisible claws dove forward and pierced her. The claws stabbed from above her collarbone and scooped the bone like two meat hooks. Her vision went black with pain as she tried to grab hold of the claws to relieve the pain. Nothing was there, her hands slapping uselessly at her own chest as her body began to slide out of the room. She grasped for the bed, but it just rolled on its wheels along with her.

Her arms swung wildly from side to side, her legs kicking out and trying to get purchase on something, anything that would stop her rapid movement toward the door. All pain in her injured leg was forgotten as her body was flooded with blind panic. Her fingers scraped against the hard tile, trying to dig into the unforgiving surface. Several of her fingernails peeled back and off, leaving bloody smears where she'd grasped for a hold as she was dragged closer to the door. The pain of losing them didn't even register; her whole world was zeroed in on the hooking feeling in her shoulders that was dragging her along the floor like a cow ready for the slaughter. Her breath was gone, and she was left with gasps that provided no relief to the agony and terror.

She tossed her head wildly in the dim light, trying to see her attacker when she could barely see the outlines of the furniture in the room. One moment, the storm cloud of smoke was on top of her, stabbing and grabbing her in every way. In the next gasping breath, it seemed like the room was empty aside from the roaring sounds in her ears. Her legs continued to kick uselessly, and she lost purchase with her bloody fingertips.

As her head was about to go through the doorway, she grabbed the doorframe hard. She held on with every ounce of power that her fever-worn body had, so that her arm muscles bulged and felt like they were going to tear apart. Her legs swung out the door, and although there should have been more floor of the hallway underneath them through the doorway, they felt like they were hanging in the open air. She kicked to try to bring them back into the room, and the pain in her injured leg bloomed into her mind again. The leg was useless with its torn muscles and damaged tissue.

Her body felt like it was going to be torn apart, collarbone caving in and pulling through her entire body. Though she didn't want to, she peeked over her shoulder into the hallway. A wispy darkness whipped around in the shadows of the hall. Gasping, she looked toward the hospital room and continued straining to hold on.

Her hands left bloody handprints on the doorframe and the tiles as she re-gripped, white-knuckled, one hand at a time until she had her elbows up on the door, as well. Though she was weak from the last few days, she pulled with all her might and wrapped herself around the door, her arms on the inside of the room and her knees tucked against the wall in the hallway. Curled up in a ball around the door, in the tightest hug of the wall she could manage. Her hands dug harder into the metal door frame, and she squeezed her eyes hard shut and panted, crying.

"Please. Please, I don't want to go! Aaghgh! I don't care if I'm the last one left. I'm not ready to go yet!" Her squeezed shut eyes leaked out more tears, and her muscles screamed at her to release the tension.

"I. DON'T. WANT. TO. GO!" she roared, her eyes squeezing so tightly shut that red fireworks were bloomed in her mind's eye. Her throat felt like it was tearing open from her screaming demand.

A second force gripped around her ankles with red-hot angry spider fingers that clamped down like irons, and her grip on the door failed. She let out the loudest scream; it felt like it was going to explode her lungs and voice box.

Everything went still then, and she was lying on the cold tile of the hallway. The presence was gone. Trembling, she pushed herself up with her bleeding fists. It was as though she had dreamed the whole thing in a red fever dream that had led her out the door. Her arms wobbled with the weight of her body, and a string of spit hung from her lip. She looked around wide-eyed, tears staining her face. All she could see was the regular gloom of the hallway and light from the windows at the end of the hall. The only thing she could hear was her own sobs, which seemed far away.

"I didn't want to go," she said to herself quietly, squeezing her eyes shut and then opening them again.

She rolled to her side and felt all over her body with panicked bloody fingers. Her hands explored her collarbone, only to find that there were no gaping wounds like she'd imagined. She looked down at her ankles, seeing nothing but bruises and cuts that had been there from before. Leaning against the wall, she heaved breath into her lungs, trying to calm herself. Every few breaths, she looked around, hoping that she wouldn't see that black shape come around the corner again. Her snot was thick and bubbling over her lips, sticking to her chin. She rubbed her arms, trying to find comfort in her own touch.

After what felt like an hour of sitting there, she managed to calm herself. Her sobs cooled down to an occasional hiccup and her heartbeat stopped hammering in her chest. Despite the hurt in her whole body, she climbed to her feet with the support of the wall. After the trauma of surviving almost being sucked out of this dimension by who knew what, she just wanted a sip of goddamned water. Limping along the corridor, she found the canteen. It smelled like dust and long-rotten food, but in the kitchen were stacks upon stacks of water, as well as the holy grail—some Gatorade. She dragged a case of water and a case of Gatorade to the closest hospital room that didn't have a reddish-brown stain on the bed and pushed them up next to the bed. Nursing the sugary drink, she gingerly climbed onto the starched white sheets and wrapped herself in the blanket that had been neatly folded at the foot. She drank four bottles of blue Gatorade while sobbing, and then threw them back up. Staring at the blue puddle on the floor, she fell asleep with her head cradled in her hands.

The gentle glow of light from the hallway roused her from her near-death sleep. Katy groaned and tried to open her eyes. Crusted shut, they had to be rubbed before they would peer open at the world. Her vomit from the night before was still sticky on the floor next to her. She stared up at the paneled ceiling and let her tears leak out until there was a cold wet spot under her head on the pillow.

Her injured leg throbbed—a bone-deep hurt. Taking small sips of air even hurt. A bottle of painkillers was only a few inches away on the table, but she could barely even tilt her head to see it. Finally, she picked them up with a shaking, bloodied hand and swallowed them dry. She went back to staring at the ceiling, feeling the pills as a hard lump in her throat. Soon after, Katy managed to curl up in a fetal position on the cot and doze for the rest of the day, ignoring her empty stomach raging against the pain pills and antibiotics.

Katy moved to the canteen the next day. The light from the wide bay of windows offered a view of a field nearby that was much more comforting than the sterile hospital rooms and surgical suites. After several days of limping around the hospital for supplies and the toilet, taking handfuls of pills and sleeping in a painkiller-induced haze, Katy started to feel better. She knew it would take a long time for her wounds to heal, but the antibiotics were fighting off the infection and she was able to bandage and stitch herself up—not that she was an expert at that. Her stitches were ragged and ugly and itched something awful. A few of the deep cuts, she left alone. The deep slice through her left nipple was one of them; she didn't want to try to sew up her own nipple. She guessed she would be covered in scars for the rest of her life. The idea didn't bother her so much, seeing as there was no one else in the world to stare at her for it.

Once the swelling had gone down in her leg, it was clear that despite some tissue damage, her bone was okay.

The scar would be with her for the rest of her life, but as long as she finished the course of antibiotics listed on the label, she would probably be fine. At least that's what she hoped. She might be slower, and even walk with a limp, but she would be okay. After having been convinced that she would die for the last few days, it turned out that she would live through this nightmare.

One morning, when she woke up from the nest of mattresses and blankets she had made underneath one of the tables in the canteen, she felt like she wanted to walk. Some crutches in a supply closet helped her swing through the halls. Her armpits ached, but it felt good to move. Katy knew it was time to move on and heal elsewhere. She'd had quite enough of her hospital stay. Most nights she woke up in terror, dreaming that the force had come back to finish the job. In those moments, she would stare at the dark doorway and shiver until she could fall asleep again. Nightmares plagued her, threatening her with the gripping force. Other nights, a fully-grown black bear would stand in the doorway, nostrils flaring until she would begin to cry and wake up gasping.

She packed up, slowly. Crutching from room to room, she gathered medications, medical supplies, and some of the last of the canned food that was in the canteen. She only took a break to indulge in a Jell-O cup she found underneath one of the shelves. Everything she wanted to bring loaded her Subaru to the brim where it sat alone in the parking lot. She was sweating as she dragged the cases of water to the car; it was starting to become brutally hot in the California Summer. *I need to get out of this heat,* she thought to herself. How nice it would be to have the cool Oregon Summer. *Maybe I should just do that. Maybe it's time to go home.*

The limitless nature of her situation often escaped her, and she would end up thinking of the tiny apartment she'd lived in before living out of a hospital. But the world was hers now.

"I could go literally anywhere, and here I am squatting like a troll in a rundown hospital," she said to herself as she pushed a crate of Gatorade farther on top of the other gear in her car to make room. She wished she still had Old Dog to talk to. Talking to a dog was a lot less strange than talking to yourself. And she knew dogs listened, at least a bit.

The car rumbled to life after coughing a few times. Her body felt like that, too. The smaller cuts had started to feel tight and itchy as they healed, and the bigger ones were still knives of pain every time something brushed against them. Her leg would keep her awake at night and make her feel woozy during the day, but the wound was healing. Healing was so much work, she found that the sun wasn't even close to being high in the sky and she already wanted a nap. She guessed life would feel like this for some time.

Sometime later, driving on I-5, she passed through the ghost town of Sacramento. Weaving around crashed cars and peering into the alleys and side streets. She stopped the car in front of a big intersection. Hauling herself up and hopping to the crutches, she then made her way to the storefront of a dry cleaner that was clearly visible. She pulled out some spray paint from her backpack and held it up. Trying to decide what to write, she hesitated with her finger on the button.

I'M STILL ALIVE - HEADED TO OREGON - NOT SURE WHERE.
CHECK MEDFORD FOR UPDATES

She watched the black paint drip on her thick letters and then got back into the car to escape the blistering heat that was starting to make the roads shimmer and glow. It hurt to sit in the car, but she drove for hours, not wanting to stop. She saw signs of life, but no human life. Cattle grazed along the road as if nothing had happened. The pastures were big enough that they were doing fine on their own, though she didn't know how long that would last without the water runoff from Winter. She thought about her sign… would anyone ever read it? Or was it a message to the dead, written by the soon to be dead?

She siphoned gas, placing the extra canisters on the rack on top of her car. The process was extra tiring, and she wondered how long she would have the luxury of doing this before the petrol degraded and her car-having days would be gone. For now, the gas still worked. She broke into a convenience store and took mini-pies, a six-pack of beer, and some chips. She then went to pee outside, rather than tolerate a non-flushing gas station toilet. She had taken to relieving herself wherever the mood took her—as long as it wasn't a toilet. She'd hated gas-station toilets when the world was alive, and now that it was gone, she might as well pop a squat in the parking lot. Squatting wasn't possible right now, though. Leaning against the outside of the building, she roughly pulled down the shorts she was wearing, kicking them away. Naked from the waist down, she spread her legs as far as she could to pee in something resembling a squat, trying not to pee on her boots.

"This is the life right here," she said to herself, tilting her hiking boot away from the stream of urine that tracked through the dust in eddies and branching rivers. She could only imagine what she looked like. Dirty, fevered, covered in ragged wounds and pissing against the side of an abandoned gas station.

Dressed once again, she tore open the wrapper of one of the gas-station pies and ate it leaning against the car, the sugar making her sigh in relief. Every thirty miles or so, she would pull the car over to rest her eyes and stretch out her aching leg. CDs kept her company. The sound of another person's voice helped an ache that she hadn't known she had. She would sing along and respond to rhetorical questions in the talk shows she found burned onto a CD from her mom that had been hidden between the seats. Her mom had had some favorites from NPR that she'd loved so much that she would listen to them more than once. She'd called it the "thinking list" and would recommend it to all of her friends—and sometimes people she barely knew. Listening to the familiar stories lulled Katy into a peaceful feeling as she tapped the steering wheel and wiggled her toes in her boots to keep them from feeling stiff. For the first time since before she'd fallen in Yosemite, she felt a little tickle of happiness.

She could only drive for a few hours at a time, though. Her body was healing, and it needed to sleep more than anything else, so for half of the day and all of the night, she would curl up in the back of the car with blankets piled up over her and rest. Some days, she wouldn't drive at all, if the ache was too great or if she found a particularly good grocery store to camp out in front of. The days were a haze of a dream that she wandered through. The sky was her blanket as she lay out in the back of the car with the seats laid flat, listening to the crickets and the occasional animal pass by.

CHILDLIKE

Katy hadn't been to Bend, Oregon since she was a child. Her memories of the place were foggy, but she remembered she liked it. The small-town feel and the lush forests surrounding the city. She remembered going on a hike with her parents, lagging behind as she stopped to look under rocks for bugs or chase lizards.

She pulled up to the sign "Now entering Bend, OR" and turned off the car. With bright red letters, she put her name and the date on the sign and then drove into town. It was her town now. Katy needed to find more food, even though her body ached and she wished for a bed. The food she had brought from Yosemite and the hospital was running low, down to the last dented cans of black beans. She craved fresh food, a salad, anything. She thought about the lush forests of Oregon and the possibility that there would be some delicious mushrooms hidden there, but her body wouldn't be able to handle a journey like that quite yet. Even short walks made her legs ache and force her to nap for hours afterward. Beans would have to do until she was on two good feet again—or could at least limp farther than she could right now.

She pulled up to a natural grocery store. Before everything had gone to shit, they'd been her favorite place to blow money when she'd had it. The stores always smelled more fresh and vibrant than the big chain grocery stores. When she pried open the front doors and limped in, though, it only smelled musty and moldy, not like she remembered. The windows were fogged over with dirt. All of the wares were still neatly placed on the shelves since there had been no one to loot or destroy anything. Only ghostly silence and dust. Some of the stores she had been to had been ransacked by animals, but local wildlife hadn't discovered this one before the food had gone bad. The hush over the aisles was haunting, and for a moment, she felt a rush of claustrophobia. What if the shadow came? Her fear of that ink cloud was worse indoors, and this place seemed like the perfect place for it to come after her again. She crouched near the front door, calming her heartbeat and willing herself to go farther into the dim interior.

A few minutes later, she calmed herself and used the windowsill to pull herself back up to stand. She flicked on the flashlight she had tucked in her back pocket. Avoiding the fresh produce section, where black, rotten steaks were sitting in the meat display and ash-piles of vegetables with colorful molds were glaring at her from the displays built out of recycled pallets, she used a cart as a crutch and limped through the aisles. Items were tossed into the cart by twos and threes. Black beans, canned vegetables, pasta. Anything that she thought would keep long and would be relatively tasty. The sound of containers rattling into the cart's bottom made the room feel more alive, something to break the echoing silence of the empty store and her footsteps on the dusty linoleum. She stopped for a moment in the canned goods aisle, letting the silence ache against her eardrums. With her still-healing leg, she kicked at a row of bottled vinegar and the bottles clattered to the ground. Then she swept her hands across more of the shelves, scooping everything to the ground. A glass bottle of syrup smashed on the ground, leaving a pool of sticky brown liquid and glimmering shards of glass. She punched through a shelf full of cereal boxes and they clattered to the ground in a pile. *Take that, ink monster*, she thought, her heart pounding not from fear now, but from indignation and excitement.

Once she was done with her ritualistic noise-making, she stopped in the beauty care section, staring at the shampoo. How she longed for a real shower, one where she could sit under steam for half an hour and scrub until she was pink and glowing. Her idle hand played with the end of her long, long braid. An idea made her light up and let go of her hair. She grabbed a bottle of shampoo and conditioner.

"Duh, why didn't I think of that sooner?" she asked herself. "Outdoors store, heeeere we come!" She had a bit more of a skip with her limping steps, imagining her future shower. While standing there wishing for running water, she'd remembered when she'd been about eight years old and her family had gone camping. In the desert of Arizona, they had hung up a shining plastic bag of water with a tube coming from it to just outside of their tent. The hot sun had warmed the water inside, and a few hours later, Katy had stood under the sun-warm water and taken one of the most satisfying showers of her life while staring out at the expanse of sand and cactus. Outdoor showers might not hold the same amount of water as the modern showers Katy had once been used to, but she knew they held enough for that lather she'd so been dreaming of.

A few hours later, with a car full of canned goods, dried foods, and a reusable solar shower, she started to cruise down the quiet main street of Bend. The car windows were rolled down, her arm dangling idly out of the driver's side, her hand tapping on the sun-warmed metal of the door. She veered around a pickup truck that had crashed into a storefront on her right and continued down the mostly empty road.

Something flashed in front of the car, and both of Katy's hands flew to the steering wheel as she slammed hard on the brakes. The car screeched, skidded a bit sideways, and came to a stop. Katy peered over the dashboard, trying to see what it was that had run in front of her and hoping she hadn't hit it. Something whirled into the side of the car in a cacophony of scratches and yips, and Katy screamed in surprise. Something bounced up and down at the place her hand had been only a few moments before. A wriggling puppy was jumping up and down at the door of the car, bright blue eyes bouncing in and out of her vision as it launched itself from the ground to the window and back down again.

As her heart rate calmed down, Katy opened the door. A young Australian Shepherd puppy gleefully jumped into her lap, spinning its paws all over her legs and the car. The dog looked to be less than a year old, by her guess, and was already over thirty pounds of squirming white and blue-gray fur. It had bright blue eyes and lips that were spotted black and pink, and a big, wet pink tongue that was licking every exposed bit of skin on Katy.

"Ow, ow, OW! Hey there!" She wrapped her arms around the excited dog as it jumped and kicked at her injured leg. Her squeeze just made it wriggle more and lick at her face. Katy laughed—the first time she had laughed in her recent memory. It was a deep belly laugh that was followed by a wave of relief. She scratched between the blue and black spotted ears of the oh-so-soft dog and let the pup kiss her as much as it wanted. Puppies had the sweetest breath, unlike their adult counterparts. To her, it always smelled kind of like sweet mint mixed with freshly dug earth after a rain.

"Where did you come from?" She held the dog away from her for a moment, checking its sex and playing with its fluffy paws. It was a girl.

The dog didn't reply, lolling a wet pink tongue from her mouth. She was probably just as happy to see Katy as Katy was to see her. Dogs did better with people around, provided they were good people. She guessed the puppy had been born right before *it* had happened, given that she was friendly and interested in humans. Katy looked around on the street to see if there were any more dogs roaming around. All she could see were the empty store-fronts and cars parked neatly on the side of the road.

"Alright, pupper." She picked her up and placed her in the passenger seat.

Using one arm to steer and the other to keep the wriggling puppy from climbing on her, Katy drove to the edge of town and into a residential area. The houses here were big, with acres of land around them. One of them would soon be home, Katy had decided. The idea of living in a town was too lonely to her, with all the buildings around her that would be silent and crumbling. No, better to be where being alone had been normal even before it had happened. And she wasn't ready for "*home*" home yet. Soon, but not yet. A pang of guilt about not driving immediately to Portland made her bite her lip for a moment, fighting off tears again. The puppy playfully growled and mouthed at her hand, though, and she forgot her troubles for a moment as she drove.

She tried a few driveways and then turned away each time when cars were parked in front. She knew that Bend was a popular second-home destination, so she hoped she could find one that wouldn't have the red spots inside. No car in a driveway meant that was far more likely.

There. A typical western-style house with pine exterior and a winding driveway. Sloping roofs and wide windows facing the nature around it. She turned the wheel and climbed the driveway. A small herd of deer sprinted away from the crackling sound of her tires on the gravel. The puppy barked madly and tried to climb out the window to follow them. The driveway was empty, even near the house.

"Shh, shh, pup." She patted the center console, and the puppy wagged her tail and stared back and forth from her to the window where she'd seen the deer disappear into the woods.

"Alright, then." With a sigh, Katy climbed out of the car and let the puppy sprint out, too. Stretching, she could feel her newly healing scars pull as she moved her body. The skin around her cuts was tight and pink, stretched against her bones and muscles. Like her skin was a pair of jeans that had gotten too tight—but she knew it would all be broken in eventually. Not quite as spry as the puppy that was sniffing the trees around the front yard and chasing the path the deer had run, she pried open the garage door of the house. No car. Luckily, the garage was the kind that had a hand-operated version from the inside so she would be able to crank it shut again. Slowly, with every muscle screaming at her, she unloaded her things in short, limping trips back and forth. The last, which came with her, was several jugs of water and the solar shower. By the time she was done, her muscles were aching and her new skin itched furiously. She gulped down some water and took a handful of pills, sitting on the front porch of the house. The view of the residential road was almost completely hidden by a copse of aspen trees. The driveway was littered with pine needles and debris from the Winter, almost concealing it completely. Katy could spy the dog in flashes of white and bluish gray between the trees around the front yard.

Once the painkillers had started to make her head buzz and the pain subside, she got up to explore her new home. Sight unseen, she had already moved her things into the garage, but she figured that wouldn't be much of a problem. The house was warm and spacious, with vaulted ceilings that the hazy afternoon light streamed through, creating beams of light that warmed the leather furniture. With a wood fireplace, too — lucky her. Not that it was needed in the middle of Summer, but if she stayed here long enough, it would be good to have. She would explore more later, though; for now, she had another mission in mind. She walked through the living room and out to the main deck, where the sunlight was calling to her. The deck looked out onto a wide valley of pine and aspen trees. Aspen appeared in patches between the pine, winding in their own secret root networks into the open fields and waving their bright green, coin-sized leaves in a rippling effect. The mid-day sun was perfectly shining, so she hung up the solar shower after carefully filling it with bottled water. She found a hook outside where the previous owners had hung a horseshoe, which was perfect for the shower. The dog had been racing around the house the whole time, but now came to her to watch what the last human on Earth was doing. She was sitting down on a lawn chair on the deck and taking a nap. The puppy launched herself onto the foot of the chair, once again jostling Katy's bad leg. She didn't mind, though; the weight of another living thing on her feet was more than she could ever have asked for. Her hand drifted to soft puppy ears.

What was the last human on Earth doing? Absolutely nothing.

She woke up with a burned sticky taste in her mouth, squinting in the almost setting sun. She groaned, which instigated a ripple of wiggles and life from the puppy that had been pacing around at the end of the lawn chair.

"Urgh, hey, pup." She patted the squirming head with her eyes still half-closed. Her ravaged leg throbbed something awful. She slowly pulled herself up out of the chair, almost tipping over while getting up. With slow, laboring steps, she walked back inside. Every step brought a new stab of pain through her leg. The bottles of pills were sprawled out on the heavy granite countertop of the kitchen, right where she had tossed them earlier. She popped the lids slowly and measured out a dose, and then sipped them down with some water. She rubbed her tongue on the roof of her mouth, trying to rid herself of the awful taste of an overslept afternoon nap.

Walking back out onto the deck, she saw the sun was dipping low on the mountained horizon, almost kissing the top row of pine trees on the ridge. The air was still warm, so Katy began to take off her clothes. She was wearing loose sweatpants, as they were the only thing she was able to manage to put on over her swollen leg. They dropped to the ground in a pile, and she gingerly took off her T-shirt, too, still mindful of her tender healing body. Standing completely naked on the exposed deck, she turned the valve on the solar shower.

The warm water felt like all the relief in the world. The heat crept from her upper layer of skin deep into her stiff muscles. The water pattered onto the deck and dripped between the gaps of the planks below. She wriggled her toes in the water and let out a luxurious sigh. The sun hid down below the trees and filtered through them, rays of fire outlining her body. *This is what heaven must be like.* She fully washed her hair for the first time in months, working up a healthy lather with the shampoo and using her fingernails to give her scalp a good scratch. As the soap rinsed down her body, it stung in every cut it touched, but it felt cleansing instead of painful. The golden and red light made her feel like a piece of glittering treasure underneath the wilderness. Hidden away from the lonely world around her. Finally washed clean after so much suffering and fear.

Long after the water had run dry from the shower, she still stood there watching as the sun disappeared behind the ridge, leaving smudges of red and pink across the horizon. The mountain air pricked her skin. The puppy lapped up the water that had pooled on the deck, wagging her tail, oblivious to the magnificent sunset and the glittering treasure of the last human.

After feeding the shepherd a random combination of crackers, beans, and some beef jerky, Katy went upstairs to dry off. The house was stocked with the biggest, fluffiest towels Katy had ever seen. She found them in the master bathroom. One of her cuts opened up and stained the crisp white towel with streaks of bright red. Snuggling into the towel and drying off her hair, she walked into the master bedroom of the house to explore before the daylight left her completely. In the warm air, the house smelled like forest, all warmed timber and stone. She noticed that there were no family pictures on the walls and very few personal items in the drawers of the bathroom. Only a few travel-size bottles of toiletries left over from hotels. She guessed this had been a second or third home for someone wealthy, someone who'd probably only come here a few times a year at most. What a waste of such a beautiful place.

Detangling her long black hair was a chore. It fought back as she gently worked a brush from the tips all the way to the top. Unwinding the more stubborn knots tugged at her scalp and made it throb, especially where the gash on the back of her head was still healing. During her time in the hospital, it had become matted, since her priority had been surviving rather than keeping her tresses in order. All of this—the shower and now grooming her hair—was giving her a warm, tickling glow in her stomach. Could it be comfort? Or happiness? Whatever it was, it felt damn good. She began to hum lightly as the last of the knots dissipated and her hair ran sleek and wet down her back.

Dropping the towel, Katy stood in front of the huge mirrors of the wardrobe. Many of the smaller cuts from her fall were healed now, leaving pink streaks across her skin. The deeper ones with stitches remained, like jagged canyons across her body. The stitches looked like little ants marching along the red lines. Stitches disgusted her; they were always angry and bristling against wounded skin. The smaller scars would probably fade to nothing with time. One deep cut started from her collarbone, then wound down through her nipple and to the middle of her stomach, and that one would stay. She directed her examination to her leg. Still red and angry, it looked like the gnarled knot of a tree, dark and raised at the center with red and smaller cuts spiraling outward. The muscle dipped inward, in a sickly way. She wondered if she would ever walk normally again, or if she would always have a slight limp. Turning sideways, she looked at how her body had changed. Her ribs showed through her skin, and her always narrow hips looked even slimmer. She didn't have a Spring/Summer plumpness; she was a wintered animal. Still, she felt proud of her lean body. Her arms looked stronger. Able, powerful. It was the first time she had allowed herself to look in the mirror for a while. Seeing herself was like greeting an old friend, familiar and exciting.

The dog nipped at her.

"Hey, pup. What's up?" She waved her hand at the dog to welcome it forward. The puppy happily bounded up to her. Her hands wound through the puppy's thick fleecy coat.

"What should I name you, friend?" She sat on the edge of the bed and patted it in a welcome sign for the shepherd to come up with her. The puppy launched toward the bed in a less than graceful bound, and Katy scooped her hind legs up so that she wouldn't tumble back to the ground.

"I was thinking New Dog... hmm. Nah. Poor Old Dog doesn't need a comparison name." The dog didn't seem interested in her naming and was snuffling at the sheets of the bed, ears flopped forward.

"Jenny." She paused. *Yeah, Jenny.* Sure, it wasn't a regular dog name, but it would be good to call out a name that sounded like a person. A certain person actually… a name she hadn't said in some time. It felt good to say it out loud. Jenny didn't respond to her new name; instead, she walked in circles near the head of the bed and flopped down on the pillows. Head on paws, she was looking at Katy with bright blue eyes.

Katy thought about Jenny. Not Jenny the dog, but Jenny the person. The one who'd gotten away—one of the ultimate human experiences. Every person seemed to recall that love that seemed perfect but didn't last, or that unrequited crush that they couldn't help thinking of from time to time. Katy and Jenny hadn't experienced a huge blow-up fight or a break-up that had broken anyone's heart, but still, it was a loss that Katy thought about often. Their love had felt so pure and sweet, unlike some of the other loves in Katy's life that had been much less innocent. If she could dream up one person that she would have loved to reconnect with, it would have been Jenny.

Katy yawned. In the dimness of twilight, still naked, she crawled under the covers. Jenny the dog sighed at the disturbance and re-settled to have her u-shaped back pressed against Katy. One arm on the fluff of the dog's back, Katy fell asleep, and into one of her first sweet dreams in months.

Katy was roused by hands on her tummy, soft and firm at the same time. She kept her eyes closed and reached out, feeling soft skin and curves next to her. A smile tugged at her sleeping lips.

"Jenny, you woke me up," she said, rolling over in her tangle of hair and bedsheets. Even with her eyes shut, she could feel Jenny smiling at her from the pillow next to her.

"Shh, if you don't open your eyes, I didn't wake you up." Jenny's voice sounded like rain on a windowpane during a drought.

"Well, if I'm talking, then I'm awake, Jenny." Katy kept her eyes closed, cupping her hands around Jenny's puppy-soft, short-cropped golden hair. Everything about Jenny had always been golden. Her hair, her skin, her voice. Jenny's hands eagerly explored her body, as well, and heat began to grow between her thighs.

"Well, be awake then." Jenny's lips met hers, sweet and soft with firmness at the end of each sweet kiss. Katy kissed back, and a shivering sigh started from her lips and ran all the way to her toes. She opened her eyes and rolled on top of Jenny.

Jenny laughed, bright white teeth flashing. Her skin was glowing so much that a haze appeared around her skin, lighting up the bedsheets. Katy placed her hands on Jenny's hips, feeling the soft curves. Soft on soft, her lower stomach tingled more as she took one thigh and placed it firmly between Jenny's legs, where she could feel a blooming warmth matching her own. She wrapped her hands around Jenny's curved hips, feeling the deep indents of the dimples at the crown of her lower back with her fingertips. Katy loved those dimples.

It was a dream want. A needful ache. A wish for those dimples above her waist, her inner thighs. A golden and thirstful itch, a sinful squish. A want that would never go away, that burned at the very pit of her stomach as they kissed and their breath grew heavy against each other's lips. A dream woven in amber and gloss; a want that didn't go away and only grew stronger and Katy pulled off Jenny's soft sleep shirt.

Katy's eyes opened, and she let out a heavy sigh. The room was empty and cold. In the mountains, even in the heat of Summer, the warmth of the day would whisk away as the sun set. Just a dream. Jenny the dog was asleep on the floor. The glowing need from her dream was still there, and she ached for her old lover again. Jenny had been a Summer fling, a girl who had only been in town to visit her family in Sacramento. Probably the most in love Katy had ever felt, and it had ended as quickly as it had begun when Jenny had moved back to Florida. They'd kept in touch over emails every once in a while, but it had been clear that the Summer would never repeat itself. Katy was pretty sure that Jenny had a boyfriend now. Well, had had a boyfriend. Despite her mind's nudging intention to remind her that Jenny was most certainly dead now, Katy fought off the morbid thought and held on to the feeling from her dream. For tonight, still in the fog of awakening, she could pretend that Jenny was just living out her life in Florida. Living out her golden life with her beautiful back dimples.

Her hand slipped under the covers, tracing her own stomach down to her thighs. Closing her eyes again, she settled into a rhythm and rocked herself to sleep, dreaming again of Jenny.

WOLF DREAM

Two states away, the wolves woke up for a night of hunting. Only a few of them had survived the culling from the two-legged ones in the last few years, but after a whole Winter of peace, they were feeling strong. The pack alpha had caught the scent of elk nearby and had roused the whole pack from their rest. Their bellies had been fat with elk meat for many weeks, and just as the hunger had touched them again, they already had a new dinner waiting for them after a long hard run. The alpha, a big wolf with a scar across his gray and black muzzle, was confident now. When the pack members were all awake, snapping at each other in anticipation, he trotted out of the den with his ears pricked forward. The night was perfect for the hunt. A brisk breeze pulled them along the scent of their quarry, and the moon lit the path beneath their feet. He knew that this Summer of plenty would not last forever and he was not so easily lulled into comfort as the younger pack members. Winter would always come again, and so could the humans. Though, the wolves had gone for so long without seeing them that the youngest pups just born had been born into a world with only the stories of their parents to remind them of those terrible creatures.

The rest of the pack followed his healthy pace out of the den and into the open fields. The elk were grazing nearby. The earth became hard and gray beneath their paws. All of the wolves out on this hunt remembered, as they had been alive many Winters, that this was the Dangerous Place. The place where they'd dared not go before. The smell of the Dangerous Place was faint now. No more acrid fuel and two-legger food. All of the fear-smells were fainter now, but still, the whites of the wolves' eyes showed as they kept alert. The elk had also noticed that the Dangerous Place was now safer and had gone to a lush field across from the strip of the hard-black path that most animals avoided. The wolves could see them now, heads dipped into the tall grass. Ears flicking back and forth as they chewed the lush green grass. The wolves fanned out, following the sharp cues from the alpha. The wolf pack's trot broke out into a sprint once their clicking claws were done crossing the road, and they moved into the tall grass from the side of the clearing where they would make their attack.

In a burst of motion, the elk scattered, zig-zagging across the field as the animals on the edges sounded the alarm that predators were there. The air was full of the hammering of hooves and the whisper of grass. An older elk tripped when he spun his long legs to get away. He was easy prey. A female wolf went in for the kill. She was young, but big and strong, and the alpha had already taken notice of her. Belly already growing fat with new puppies, she sank her teeth into the neck of the elk.

Blood rushed around her jaws and whet her growing appetite. She kept her bite strong and gave the neck a good shake. The elk gurgled and moaned as it attempted one last bugle call to its herd. But the other elk were already long gone, leaving the wolves with their prize. The alpha walked over to the female proudly, sinking his teeth into the elk, as well. It was a good evening to laze in the field and gorge themselves beneath the blanket of stars.

As the elk re-formed their herd, they found that without their oldest member, they were faster now. A healthy group that would be able to run farther and graze more. The price to be paid for keeping the rest of the herd safe. They dipped their heads in homage to their fallen friend and moved to other fields. Settling down near a trickling creek, the elk continued to graze, keeping one eye always on the edges of the field for more gray-furred danger.

A fat beaver watched her new elk neighbors with disinterest before gnawing hard on the tree in front of her. Only a little more work and it would topple down with a crash, which would scare all of the elk into a stampede again. The creek had begun to build up into a pond behind her—her hard work of chewing, felling trees, and then bringing them to her dam was paying off. The pond had begun to grow since early that Summer. Enough time that a thick layer of sediment had built up at the bottom. That sediment attracted bugs and bacteria, which fed the fish that had found themselves in deeper waters instead of down the creek. The fish were plentiful in the deep waters of the pond. A perfect hunting ground for the birds of prey and other small predators. The beaver used her strong front teeth to saw away at the tree, digging her claws into the earth for purchase as a hawk settled down in the trees above to rest for the night. She was the creator of habitat, of life. Her home was also the home of all of these new animals. The neighborhood architect.

The air felt cleaner to these animals, even though they couldn't understand or explain why. The nights were quieter, safer. The great fear of the inescapable two-legged-standing-things was starting to fade from their memories. Some of the animals born that Spring knew nothing of this fear, except for what had been instilled in their parents since they still distrustfully avoided the abandoned homes and cities. It would be some time until the more skittish species would take up residence in those places again. They still felt too foreign, cold, and devoid of food. The only animals that had already found paradise in these places were the raccoons, rats, and coyotes. They were always the first movers, finding comfort in all places and resources in all places. Now, they had a kingdom to themselves, even though it was barren of the delicious garbage they'd once been used to. Treats still lingered inside of some of the big concrete buildings. Spring had brought a surge in growth, even in the barren concrete human places. In a few years, their buildings would be split apart from new saplings and plants. The wild would retake these artificial castles.

In the sudden silence of the world that Winter, life had continued as it always had. The earth still orbited the sun, and Winter had made way to Spring and then to Summer.

Humanity was gone, and the earth didn't care.

RABBIT-SHAPED BOX

After two weeks of resting in her peaceful mountain home, Katy's body was beginning to heal. Her time had been spent sleeping, getting to know Jenny, and ferrying supplies back and forth from town. As her body got stronger, she found more energy to fret and worry. Now, without imminent death keeping her distracted, her mind continued to wander to the darkness in the hallway.

One night, she settled into bed long after the sun had set. In the darkness of the room, she was hyper-aware of Jenny shifting and settling at the foot of the bed. She felt on edge and mentally punished herself for not visiting her parents yet. She mourned JD and Danielle, and even Tim a little bit. She missed them. She also wondered why her bloody noses had stopped as soon as everyone had gone "pop." Her thoughts had her tossing and turning. When she finally fell into sleep, she was sucked into an unwanted dream.

The walls were closed in around her, metal and cold. There was nowhere for her to rest in her box-shaped cage. The hard floor hurt her paws, and the food tasted strange. Trying to get comfortable, rabbit-Katy scratched at the stainless steel.

She could hear other rabbits thumping around above and below her. All of them felt trapped. She stared out of the bars of her prison, to the yellow-lighted room where she watched the humans experiment on other animals. No one was there to torment the rabbits or rats at the moment. She tried to lie down and stretch out in the cage.

Human voices came from outside of the room, and her ears perked up to listen as the voices got closer. They sounded angry. The door burst open, and rabbit-Katy jumped away in horror. It was her! Human-Katy stood in the lab, arguing with someone outside of the door. The someone walked in, imposing, towering over little human-Katy. It was Mr. Harris, the security agent. He shouted at human-Katy, and rabbit-Katy watched helplessly. She couldn't understand the words they were saying, only the tone of voice. Rabbit-Katy dug at the corner of her cage, trying to shake the door loose.

She was interrupted by the sound all rabbits fear—a death scream. All of the rabbits to the right of her began to scream, jumping and bashing themselves against their cage walls. She shied away to the corner, as far away as she could get from the terrible sounds. Looking out, she saw Mr. Harris clap his blue-gloved hands over his ears, and so did human-Katy. The two people began to scream, too, their eyes wide but unseeing. Blood ran from their noses into their open yelling mouths. Rabbit-Katy's sensitive rabbit ears hurt at the sound, but she did not cower away. She couldn't stop watching as a dark cloud burst into the room from the hallway.

Human-Katy had her eyes wide open and had fallen to her knees, her hands clapped over her ears with her fingernails digging into her own head. Mr. Harris had fallen unconscious next to her. The cloud hovered and pooled over the ceiling above the humans—and a vibrating hum buzzed through the air. Rabbit-Katy watched as her human body burst at the seams, exploding across the room. Mr. Harris also ballooned up and exploded. Blood spattered across the neat lab tables and the white linoleum floor. A human ear splattered against the grate of her cage.

The smoke slithered down the wall near the door, becoming more solid as it filled the doorway.

"NO!" As rabbit-Katy screamed, the smoke turned to look at her. For just a moment, the smoke looked like a stag's head. A red, glowing third eye burned into rabbit-Katy as she tried to kick open the cage.

Katy gasped awake, pushing herself up on the pillows.

"What the fuck!" She huffed. She'd had nightmares before, but none like that. Her hands wound around the soft sheets, twisting and squeezing them.

"It felt so real. It wasn't real, it wasn't real," she muttered to herself. Jenny stood up from where she'd been sleeping near the doorway of the bedroom and wiggled at her. The dog's cheerfulness just soured her fear even more.

"No, Jenny. No, Jenny, not now." Katy couldn't kick the fear from the dream. She felt like she was still trapped in that cage, watching herself get pulled to pieces.

Katy never rid herself of the feeling of that dream. And the fear began to haunt her during the day as her mood soured. The hope she had felt when she'd first come to Bend began to run dry.

DESPERATION HAS A SCENT

"FUCK, FUCK, fuck, fucking fuck this!" She threw a mug against the wall in the kitchen. It exploded into pieces and flew across the tile floor. Jenny tucked her tail and ran under the table, peering at Katy from her hiding place. Katy had been sitting at the big oak dining room table, the world spinning around her. When she'd felt like she was about to tumble down into a hole of madness and never be able to climb back out, she had thrown the mug in a desperate attempt to release the discontent building up inside of her. The last piece of the mug skittered to a stop against the useless dishwasher, and Katy stayed frozen on her chair, hand still held open for a mug that was no longer there. Her act of violence had stopped the feeling that the world was tipping out of her control, the floor becoming the ceiling and the ceiling the floor. Now, she sat in the aftermath.

She collapsed on the floor of the kitchen and began scooping up the shattered pieces, letting the hard tile bite into her knees as she crawled from piece to piece. Jenny stayed under the table, staring at the human who had exploded for seemingly no reason.

Katy hadn't been sleeping, instead pacing back and forth in the bedroom. Dark circles under her eyes grew darker and puffier. When she slept, dreams haunted her. Dreams of touching, dreams of being completely alone forever, dreams of strange and faraway places. Dreams of a bear, or the white room, or being dragged into the void by invisible hands. Dreams of the stag with the third eye.

Now, the dreams haunted her even when she was awake. It didn't matter if she avoided sleeping. The black smoke would descend on her, only for her to scream and tear away to see nothing. When she wasn't seeing things, she was surrounded by a lonely desperation that ate away at every moment. Other things had been hard since it had happened, and sometimes she'd had a day where all she could do was cry in bed, but this was a whole new level of desperation.

"I can't do this!" she sobbed as she hugged the pieces of the mug to her chest, kicking her legs out from underneath her to sit on the hard tile floor.

The dog tentatively wagged her tail in wide, low sweeps and walked toward Katy. Katy dropped the pieces of the mug from her hands and opened her arms. Jenny walked into them, still shaking. Katy stroked the dog, and Jenny licked her face. The soft wet tongue on her salty cheek woke her up a little bit.

"I'm so sorry, Jenny girl. I'm just so lonely." She hugged the dog close for a moment and then stood up. The process of sitting down and standing up was more fluid as her injury healed and her muscles began to knit together again. She had spent time bending it and strengthening the leg. What else was she going to do?

Sometimes doing the exercises and massaging the stiff leg would make her grimace in pain, but it reminded her that she was alive and gave her something to fret over other than the thoughts that felt maddening.

"You don't know what it's like. There are other dogs in the world still, good things to sniff, and still one human for you. I never gave that much of a shit about people, but now that they're gone, all I want is someone to talk to. You know?" She tugged on Jenny's blue and black spotted ears and Jenny sighed, enjoying the positive attention.

Katy sat there for what felt like a few minutes, staring at the refrigerator. This house was everything she could have dreamed of in her normal life. An escape in the mountains with a stable in the back (empty—she had checked). Neighbors half a mile away or more, and near a town that had everything she needed and no more. Now, it felt hollow. Her plans had never included a partner to share her life with, but now that there was no one to even talk to at the grocery store (or even a grocery store to browse), she wondered why it was worth it at all. She had furiously cleaned away the grime and dust in this house, only to pretend like she just didn't feel like going into town and seeing people. Like everything was normal.

The silence of no fridge-hum, no lights to switch on, and no appliances to conveniently cook on ruined that perfect lie.

Jenny got up and walked to the back door and whined, looking at Katy. Katy sighed, brushed off her palms, and got up to let her outside. Jenny trotted out and down the side stairs onto the back lawn. Katy followed. She walked out of the open door, barefoot and topless. In the Summer heat, it was much more comfortable to forgo a shirt. She remembered her mom pulling her aside when she'd been a little girl and telling her that she needed to wear a shirt outside from then on. She hadn't understood it then, and now there was no one to tell her that a lady needed to cover up. Cover up what?

Down the stairs and onto the dry grass, Katy hung onto the sensation of the sticks and plants pressing into her bare feet. Anything to feel grounded. The world did a spin as she looked at the horizon and squinted, shook her head, and took a deep breath. She wandered around the side of the house and found herself standing on the driveway, letting the hot concrete burn her feet.

The dusty Subaru sat outside, unused for a week. She climbed in, and Jenny hopped into the passenger seat like she had when they'd first met. Katy took the keys from where she left them, the center console, and started the car and drove. With the windows rolled down, the tires kicked up dust as they rolled into town. Main Street, empty and lonely. Katy parked in the middle of the road. She strolled down the sidewalks, window-shopping. Stores of souvenirs for tourists, empty bars, a laundromat with the window shattered. She paused at a craft store and recalled her full sketchbook at home. She had covered every inch of it with writings and sketches. She needed a new one.

The first waft of air from the shop smelled musty from having been closed up for almost a year now. Katy set her crowbar down and took a look around the store. Everything was in its place, canvases stacked neatly on the shelves, with only a layer of dust to give away that there had been no shoppers. Katy stopped at the cashier's desk and adjusted a wooden posing figure into another shape, and then she picked up a shopping basket. With the basket hanging neatly in the crook of her arm, she walked down the dark aisles, pointing her flashlight at the canvases and notebooks to get a better look. Jenny followed closely behind, sniffing around the rows before lying down on the cool tiles near the front door, her bright pink tongue lolling out of her mouth.

A while later, Katy left the store with a stack of blank canvases and notebooks, as well as several tubes of paints. She carefully closed the door to the store, as she didn't want bad weather or animals spoiling her personal art supply. As she was arranging her shopping wares in the back of the car, head ducked under the back door, something caught the corner of her eye, just a few feet away at the corner of the street. The shadow grew, standing tall on its hind legs, big paws hanging to its sides. Just as the bear materialized to full size, Katy screamed and fell backward, hard. Her mind flashed to falling down the slope in the mountains, crashing into rough bark and rocks, bouncing downward like a helpless doll. Her leg was stabbed with pain again, and she crawled backward on the raw palms of her hands, blinded by her fear.

There was nothing there. No bear. Nothing but the same quiet street and blue sky. Jenny poked her head around the corner of the block to look at her with her ears perked forward. Trembling, Katy climbed to her feet again. A twinge in her bad leg pinched hard, clamping down onto her newly vulnerable muscles. Swearing, she limped into the car and whistled for Jenny. Jenny ran up and into the open passenger side, and Katy leaned over and slammed the door shut. Her hands were slick with sweat on the steering wheel as she started the car.

On the drive home, there were a few times where she could have sworn she saw the back end of a bear disappearing into the forest. Her hands would grip the steering wheel hard, hard enough to hurt to wake herself up and out of seeing such things. Every time, the vision disappeared as quickly as it had come, and every time, it left without a threat. Still, she couldn't help but feel like she was going to be torn away from her new life by the black shadow of the hospital.

When she was back at the house, she swept everything off the dining room table and spilled out the contents of the art store. Brushes, tubes of paint, and pencils all clattered across the knotted pine table. Sitting down, she opened up a sketchpad and took one of her favorite brands of black ballpoint pens and began to draw. The meat of her hand pressed hard into the paper, and her lines showed up dark and heavy. An ear began to emerge, and a long nose. She drew how she remembered Old Dog—tongue out, looking up at her adoringly.

Her hand was smudged with the ink when she flipped the page and started anew. The sketches poured out of her like she was dumping out the pitchers of her hurt and loneliness. It felt good, even as her hand cramped and her shoulders ached from hunching over the pages. Soon, she noticed that she was squinting to see the pages and Jenny was whining at her food bowl. Sitting up, her muscles protested, cramped. Rubbing her back, she stood and realized that the sun had already gone down; she had been trying to see in the twilight.

The dog food clattered noisily into the empty bowl and Jenny gobbled it up, wagging her fluffy round Australian Shepherd butt back and forth as she did so. Katy padded back over to the table and sat down, pulled back into her drawing. The candles she lit shrunk shorter and shorter, and one of them began to pool wax on the table. She couldn't stop, though. Every time she thought about it, she imagined seeing that hulking lump of fur in the corner of her eye, rearing up. Her art was the spell she was casting to keep the monsters at bay. If she stopped, her protective wards would be gone. The glow of morning before the sun came, and it replaced the candles as two of them burned out forever. Jenny would come and wind around Katy's legs on occasion, yearning for affection and then giving up to retire to the plush bed that Katy had taken from a pet store in town.

After two days more of feverish drawing, only interrupted by letting Jenny out or feeding her, Katy ran out of paper and canvas. Eyes bloodshot, she sat in the chair and tried to still her hands that were still twitching and quivering to draw. She saw the open white wall of the dining room. Yes, her next canvas. She hauled out a can of black paint she'd remembered seeing in the garage and pried open the can with a kitchen knife. The paint went thick and glistening onto the pristine white wall. First using brushes and then her fingers to draw out her story, Katy painted. Her eyes felt tired and dry, and the whole world thrummed with her need for sleep. The paint was cool and wet on her fingers, and the rhythm of brushing it onto the wall kept her in a trance. Hours later, when she stumbled away to look at her work, finally she knew she could rest. Hand tired, hanging at her side and dripping paint onto the white carpet. A bear towered over the dining room table now, all shadows and mist. Clawed feet held high, towering over a ledge where a small bundled character cowered. *Her.* The bear was her, and the girl hiding from the bear was her. Maybe the black smoke in the hospital was real, or maybe it wasn't. Maybe it was also some part of her. But the bear, the bear was merely a figment of her imagination. Her fear wrapped into a more tangible form. She understood the pain and suffering, and she accepted it. She accepted the aching loneliness and the fear. And she was convinced that her ritualistic painting had finally chased away the dark shadows for good.

Her work finally done, she stumbled upstairs. Clumsy, sleep-deprived, she used one of the expensive plush towels folded neatly in the closet to wipe her hands of the black paint, and she left it crumpled like a newspaper on the bathroom floor. She climbed into the big empty bed, wrapping the blankets around her and imagining she was a bat wrapped in her own leathery wings.

In the morning, she would fly.

That night, she dreamed of Jenny the lover again instead of facing twisted nightmares.

The Summer was light and airy still, like an idea that had just started to form. Changeable, but warmer than Spring. It was already beginning to cool off in the afternoon, despite the fact that the sun hadn't begun to set. She was in an old rental apartment from a few years back. She paced back and forth, glancing at the clock and then at all of the snacks she had arranged on a tray on the coffee table. Katy had laid out a feast for them, with strawberries and cheeses. With a nervous hand, she adjusted the roses in the vase next to the platter. A knock at the door made her jump, and she ran to answer it. There she stood, Jenny, wearing a short Summer dress. The floral kind that would tousle just right in the breeze to reveal the high, secret place of a woman's thigh.

Katy brought her into a warm hug and kissed her cheek. Her cheeks were always so soft, smooth, with little fuzzy white hairs that you could see when she was backlit. Like a little peach. Jenny's eyes lit up when she saw the roses on the table and the snack plate.

"Oh, Katy!" Jenny kissed her back again, eagerly, and then explored the gifts that Katy had laid out.

"There's more," Katy said, reaching out to lead Jenny to the balcony.

"What else!?" She followed.

"You'll see." Katy opened the door. She had placed a warm, soft blanket on the paved balcony, with some pillows and two glasses. With a perfect view out on the world below them.

They settled down there, naked. Wrapped up in blankets. The apartment was on the top floor, so no one else could see them having their secret meal. Katy smiled and laughed as Jenny threw olive pits off of the balcony onto the path below and then ducked away from the edge, hiding from her own mischief. Katy could live in the moment forever, looking at Jenny's soft golden hair falling into her face as she pulled the blankets around her. Naked, but also protected.

"You know, it's okay, Katy." She was staring at Katy with her big blue eyes.

"What's okay?" Katy asked, popping another olive into her mouth.

"The world will be okay, okay? And so will you," Jenny said, smiling.

Katy pulled Jenny into her arms and leaned against the wall, letting Jenny's head rest on her shoulder. She stroked Jenny's bare arms with her fingertips and kissed the top of her head.

Maybe everything would be okay.

BAT SONG

The bats jostled each other in their roosts, a quivering mass of thousands and thousands with wings like leathery blankets to hide them from the daylight. The sun was getting low in the sky. Not time yet, but almost. Close enough that they were re-gripping their feet on the underside of the bridge, chirping at their neighbors. Hopefully, there would be good bugs—yes, many bugs. The stagnant pools, ponds, and irrigation ditches that had been left to grow algae and dirt during the Spring had been a birthing ground for more mosquitoes than usual. The bats were fat, but they were always hungry.

A young bat stretched her wings, letting out a big yawn. Her snout stretched wide open, showing the bright white spikes of her teeth. Her neighbor, poked by her wings and small grasping hands, also began to stretch and yawn.

Time? he chirped, re-gripping one clawed foot and the other, peering down with his almost blind eyes at the river.

Yes, she replied by flapping her wings and spinning on her roost. *The bugs are out, the river is full of them. Tasty, tasty.*

He nodded in agreement. The bats closer to the edges began to drop from their roosts, and after a few moments of free fall, they spread their strange mammal wings and flapped into the night, chirping their way through the air. Every chirp returned to their rotating, thin ears. The world was a picture painted with sound. A world with bugs!

The young female let go with her tiny grasping feet, falling face-down into the air. The exhilaration of moving after the day of sleep made her giddy, and she let out an extra-loud chirp. The older bats around her grumbled in their half-asleep, half-awake state, but she didn't care. Chirping her way through the air, she dove low, wings almost touching the river below her that was fat and lazy with water. A bug practically flew right into her mouth. She crunched it up, slurping the good juices and tasting the good legs. *Now, more.*

Her roost-mate joined her, chirping against the water and the world around him. He also found good bugs. They would fly many miles and eat many good bugs tonight. This, she could tell. It was a good night for bugs. The day had been hot and sticky, and the bugs were hungry for their own food, as well. Many animals were still there for them to feed on, but some of their favorites were gone, so they searched longer and harder, only to be eaten by the happy bats. So many mosquitos had been born in this urban forest, but this year, there were less humans to feed on. Unlucky for the mosquitos, lucky for the bats.

A mosquito was hovering around a car that had crashed into the side of the bridge, smelling the old blood in the seat, deciding whether there would be anything good to stick her needle into. The thought ended as a hot, wet bat mouth sucked her up.

Good, she said after slurping down the last leg that had been hanging out of her lips.

Yes, her roost-mate agreed as he found another mosquito considering the car.

Soon, she was feeling fat and heavy with bugs. On a whim, instead of flying back to the bridge to rest, she flew through the empty buildings. Reflective and hard-sounding when they came back to her ears. Smooth, and with no good crunchy bugs in them. The buildings echoed with her chirps, one of the only sounds in the empty city. Something was missing from here, but she was almost too young to understand what it was. The older bats talked of the slow, naked things that bugs liked to fly around. The slow, naked things were gone, they said. She didn't know about these slow, naked things—only good bugs and the bridge that was home. The moonlight reflected off of the gleaming glass. The small world of cars and once neatly-trimmed trees lining the streets that now had leaves littering the ground and grass bursting between the seams of the concrete.

After touring a bit farther into this seemingly endless jungle, the bat turned around, still listening to the echo of her own chirps. She found her way back to her roost.

Other insect-fattened bats had also arrived back at the roost, once again jostling for the best spot and flapping their wings against each other. They described the bugs they had eaten and reported the locations, as well as anything else notable. One of the most important updates was that an owl was lurking in a nearby tree. *Silent death*, they warned. The young bat wasn't worried about silent death right now, though, as her almost blind eyes closed and she relaxed in her roost. The river flowed beneath the colony that lived under the bridge and the first rays of sunlight glimmered off of the eddies and small rapids. She nestled next to her roost-mates.

Goodnight.

THE HUNT

The buck was walking gingerly through the overgrown grass beyond the deck, lifting up each cloven hoof and carefully placing it down again as it grazed. His eyes were almost shut as his black nose disappeared in clumps of green. Katy had locked Jenny in the house that morning, and the dog had fallen asleep in her bed near the back door. Katy was lying on her stomach on the deck, perfectly still behind a toppled lawn chair. The rifle was resting on top, and Katy's hands quivered at the trigger. She was afraid of the gun—always had been afraid of them. She wore earplugs and eye protection. Her eyes were on the deer only, about forty feet away, as it nibbled on the dewy grass. Down the long straight barrel, the gun was pointing like a line to the chest of the young animal. At least, she hoped it was.

She was so afraid of this moment. She could feel her palms, sweaty and slippery, as she tried to count through the checklist of things she needed to do to make a good shot. It had taken her weeks to work up to trying to take a shot at a living target. She had been practicing at the shooting range she'd found at the end of town, and every time she got ready to put her finger on the trigger, it shook. So far, she hadn't gotten used to it, and she figured she never really would. What if she missed and only injured the deer? Or what if she missed and never got to taste fresh meat ever again?

Taking a long quiet breath in and calming her thoughts, Katy pulled the trigger, and despite her practice, her eyes squeezed shut as she anticipated the noise and the kick. The gun bounced back into her shoulder; she guessed there would be an angry bruise there later. Her grip was probably all wrong. Jenny started barking excitedly at the door. Peering over the chair and setting the gun down, Katy looked to the deer. It was lying on the ground. Her fears of only injuring the beast were soothed, and she removed the earplugs and walked slowly toward her prey.

He was still breathing thick and wet bloody breaths. Blood flowed, quick and crimson from the wound onto the grass that the deer had been eating only a few seconds before. One wide black eye looked up at her, white showing around it. Katy felt a predatory hunger, mixed with guilt and pity. It was complicated.

"I'm sorry." She walked closer. The deer struggled a bit, kicking its long legs into the grass and trying to get a purchase to get up. The head came up for a moment, and it moaned, but the efforts to get away were weak at best, and it fell back again. Careful to avoid the flailing hooves, Katy approached the head, which was tilted back now, neck at an odd angle. Crouching down, she came closer to the deer. She took the knife from the clip on her belt and pressed it against the warm neck. The fur wasn't as soft as she had imagined and was almost bristling, trying to defend the deer from the knife that was pressed against its gurgling veins. Katy grunted and sliced, and blood bloomed beneath her fingertips and the steel, hot and sticky. The light started to fade from those big black eyes.

"Goodbye, horned one." She looked into his eyes one last time. Now came the harder part. Katy sheathed the knife after wiping it on the deer's haunch. Jenny was still barking wildly, tail waving like a helicopter. *I'll let you out in a minute*, Katy thought to herself as she stood over her kill.

Katy grabbed the deer's back legs. It was a young buck but still outweighed her by two times or so. At first, she didn't think she would be able to move the animal at all as she gripped the hard, wiry hind legs. She strained and the body started to drag through the grass and pine needles that littered the yard. She only had a little way to go to reach the deck. The veins in her neck stood out, bright against her skin as she grunted and pulled. Her feet dug into the grass and left imprints where she and the animal passed. The deck was a good six feet off the ground, so when she was close, she tied a rope around the hind legs of the deer and carried the rope up the stairs. She hoped the railings could hold the weight as she tossed the rope back down, through the posts and to the ground. With the makeshift winch, she hauled the deer up, dribbling blood into the dirt below. After tying off the ropes against the deck posts, she hurried back down the stairs with a bucket to place underneath the loose dangling head. The velvety antlers were scratching lines back and forth in the dirt as it swung.

She let Jenny out, and the dog eagerly ran toward the deer. The dog began lapping up the trail of blood in the grass and wagging her rump furiously. A pink foam began to grow at her jowls, flipping up and spraying as she tossed her head left to right, smelling for more blood. Strings of drool hung in loops at her lips, and one stuck into the proud white fur of her chest.

Now, that's a sight, Katy thought to herself. Looking down, she saw that she herself was also covered in blood and coarse deer hair. *This is probably a sight, too.* She took out the knife again, resting a hand on the firm body of the buck. It was still warm under her rough palm.

Katy took a book she'd left on the deck earlier and opened it next to her work station. "How to Field Dress a Deer." Katy fumbled with the knives as she read along and followed the instructions. She had found the book in the gun shop, along with the sharp hunting knives she was using now. As she stood there reading, the Summer air felt good, the smell of the forest was so strong. For a moment, Katy swore she could smell everything, as though a superhuman (or dog) sense of smell was being granted to her by a higher power. The bright, sharp blood of the deer that was starting to coagulate at the bottom of the bucket, for one thing. She could smell Jenny's shit at the edge of the lawn, even though it was from early that morning, as the breeze blew in Katy's direction. Jenny smelled coppery and comforting with that good dog stink. She wondered if this was how it felt to be Jenny. Smelling everything at once. The hair on her arms stood up as she took another deep breath in. Just as quickly as the smells had come on, they disappeared, and she was back to her ordinary senses.

Shaking her head out of the world of smells, she stood up.

"That was weird," she said to Jenny, and mostly to herself. The dog wasn't listening, instead gnawing at a stick and eyeing the corpse that was dangling from the deck, mouth still lined with bloody pink foam.

With the help of her instruction book, Katy managed a rough job of butchering the deer. The hide was tough and thick, and she struggled to make the incisions with her clumsy, unpracticed hands. She had to stand on a chair she took from the kitchen to reach the upper legs. Once the incisions were made, she began to tug and peel back the skin. It came off like a big heavy blanket once she had separated the layers of tissue and fat.

"If I knew how to tan, I could make a really great rug," she said, admiring her work before going up the stairs and hanging the pelt over the deck.

Katy felt fatigued, her muscles throbbing. It was hard work to cut up the deer, and her arms tingled from being held over her head, but she kept cutting. With one slice, the belly bloomed open and the guts fell out with a wet "plop." She didn't stop Jenny when the dog ran over and started to wolf down the entrails, eating fast—likely afraid she would be ordered to stop. The inside of the deer was still hot. Even on this warm Summer day, a bit of steam rose from the carcass. Katy's cuts were sloppy; she was no professional butcher, not with her arms covered in blood and gristle past the elbow, and blood dripping down her topless front. The blood covered her breasts in a blanket of sticky red. A fearsome look, indeed, that of the huntress.

"Enjoy. You better not barf on the carpet later," she told Jenny, who was still gobbling down every piece that Katy dropped on the ground. Wagging furiously, she made a smacking sound with her wet dog lips whenever too much time passed in between a chunk falling to the ground.

Katy pulled out the heart, holding it in her small hands. Only half an hour ago, this heart had been pumping blood through the whole body of a powerful, live deer. Now it sat heavy in her cupped hands. It was actually quite beautiful, to see all the structures like this. She pointed them out in her head. *Right ventricle. Left ventricle.* Tracing the veins and openings with her fingers. Jenny whined.

"Not for you." Katy placed it carefully in the cooler next to her. Other organs went into the large cooler, too, as well as tendons. She tried to salvage as much as she could. Big bones for stew wouldn't keep long, but maybe she could save them for a while if she could figure out how to keep them cool. She still had so much to learn about surviving in this new world.

That night, she built a big fire at the fire pit she'd found in the backyard, close to where the deer had lost his life earlier that day. She roasted a huge steak of venison over the fire, as well as many strips of meat, salted heavily. A big portion of the venison would become jerky, so that she could eat it for longer. Another helpful tip from her field dressing book. Jenny was curled up to her next to the fire, fat and happy. Katy was using a plush blanket from inside to wrap her arms as the night cooled off. The comfortable body-hum of a long day of work and the warmth of the fire soothed her almost to sleep as she watched the meat cook. Occasionally, the wind would pick up and the smoke would blow into her eyes and face. Katy would tilt her head away and let the smoke scent her hair.

Through the smoke and flames dancing across her vision, Katy could see something in the pines on the other side of the fire. It moved between trunks of red-barked pine trees, hiding itself mostly from view. The big round shape was a curious bear. This time, the bear was real. After Katy shook her head, and pinched her cheeks hard, the reflective eyes still didn't go away. The bear didn't get any closer, though, and only watched from the trees. The pair stared at each other for some time through the fire. Both enjoying the smell of cooking meat. The dog didn't seem to notice, absorbed in a big meaty bone.

Katy didn't feel afraid. Not like she had when the nothingness had tried to rip her from her bed, or when she'd stumbled into the bear at Yellowstone. The dancing bears in the corner of her vision scared her. This black bear watching her cook didn't scare her. Maybe she was getting stronger. Maybe she would be able to stay in this world a little longer without going mad, as long as she kept herself busy. She had always believed people when they'd said that humans took meaning from life by sharing it with other people. And that was true… she knew that there was something missing that she would never recover. But maybe it wasn't the only way. After all, she wasn't actually alone. Jenny's thick-furred tail was draped over her dirty, bare feet, and a pair of glowing green eyes were watching her from across the fire. She was far from alone. Keeping secret council across the flames.

The bear took one last longing look at the meat and turned back into the forest.

With her stomach bulging with warm, fresh meat and the fire down to coals and ash, Katy stood up and stretched out her stiff body. She called for Jenny and climbed the stairs to the house. The walls, painted with her dreams and thoughts, looked down on her as she entered the bedroom. She peered out the window to watch the bear emerge from the trees and sniff around the backyard.

She fell asleep smelling of woodfire and meat, satisfied and comforted by the warmth of Jenny's back pressed against her in the king-sized bed. Her full belly sent her into a deep sleep full of dreams.

The weather was gray, wet, and cold. Like it often was in Portland, especially in the Winter. The gray settled like a blanket over everything. Muting emotion and creating a sleepy feeling over the low-light days. Katy walked through the wet, cold grass barefoot. Her feet kicked up cool droplets onto her ankles and calves. She recognized the field, near her childhood home. The edges of the field were draped with a low mist. She was walking toward a figure sitting at the edge of the woods in the grass, cradling something in his massive arms.

"JD." She'd said his name not in a questioning way, knowing that it was him.

JD looked up at her and smiled. He was holding a bright white rabbit in his arms. The rabbit was wiggling its little pink nose, its blank beady eyes staring in opposite directions.

"Hey, Kitty Kat!" His voice rang through the dark quiet of the forest.

"Hey, JD. I've missed you." She sat down in the grass with him, stroking the soft back of the rabbit.

JD frowned. "You just saw me yesterday." He offered her the rabbit to hold, and she shook her head.

"I guess time has passed differently for you, then." She kept looking down at the rabbit, trying to ignore the welling tears in her eyes.

"Look, Kat." JD's hand went to her chin, tugging it gently upward.

"Don't." She let a tear tumble down her cheek.

"It's alright, look, I'm happy. Why aren't you happy?" He gave her a wide smile.

"I don't feel scared anymore, but what am I supposed to do here?" Her voice cracked and had gotten higher-pitched.

"No one knows those answers. Did they ever?" He nodded knowingly. His hand was still on her chin. The pressure and warmth felt good. Katy closed her eyes and tilted her face closer to his.

"Look. I spent all of my time in a windowless laboratory. I love animals, but I spent every day hurting them because it was the only way that I could keep studying animals and support my family." He jostled the rabbit in his arms like a baby. "The world isn't fair, and we do what we have to. It hurts most of the time."

Katy looked away, watching the trees move in the breeze. Wet streaks of rain began to dampen her hair. "It's raining." It was all she could bring herself to say.

"It always will." JD smiled again, holding out the rabbit.

Katy took it in her arms, pressing the warm plush fur to her chest.

"It always will."

BEAR DREAMS

The smell of the raw red meat drew the young male bear from behind the cover of the trees. Strings of drool dripped from his round jaws as he sniffed. He nibbled at some of the gristle left behind. The strange creature hadn't shouted or chased him away, and he had watched because the smells were so good, and strangely familiar. The human wasn't like the other ones he had seen before. She smelled different and moved differently. He felt safe sitting by the smoking remains of her fire on his back haunches, gnawing at the bone the dog had foolishly left behind.

He knew much of the human-kin. His mother had taught him that they kept dens that had tasty food left outside, and that if you tipped over their bins, all sorts of rich foods could be found. His mother had been taken by the humans, and he had never seen her again.

This year, there'd been no tasty garbage to eat. He had become hungry and left their territory. The other bears in the forest weren't happy about him coming into their land, but there were berries and bugs and many other good things to eat here. He'd managed to defend a small stretch of land and make it his.

He had heard this human-kin earlier in the day and had been watching ever since. She had a loud barker with her. Many times, he had been chased by the barkers during the seasons when the humans wore bright vests and stumbled through the woods. He chewed thoughtfully. As thoughtfully as a bear ever could. Once he was satisfied that there weren't any other pieces of food left out, he went to lick the deep and rich blood-soaked earth underneath the deck.

He was a big youngster, more brown than black in color with a luxuriously thick coat. Soon, the females would find him very attractive—yes, indeed. He was good at finding berries and dead things to eat, and he was a proud, big bear. When he was satisfied with the meal he'd been gifted, he got up and trundled back into the forest. The nighttime sounds all around him made his fluffy round ears twitch this way and that. An owl flew silently overhead and landed with a loud squeak of death as he closed in on a mouse he had been stalking. The bear's paws crunched on the leafy undergrowth, and he gave a wide berth to a fat porcupine that was grumbling to itself and walking along, sniffing at bushes and roots. He didn't want to have a nose full of quills; he had learned that lesson long ago. Some animals were good to eat, and others weren't. The porcupine didn't even look up from his scavenging as the bear passed.

The porcupine was unconcerned with stupid bears and stupid wolves. The young ones would usually try to take a chomp out of him, but it only took one try for them to learn, and the chomps never hurt him. The berries and other goodies hidden around the roots of trees were much more interesting to him. It had been a while since a stupid young animal had bitten him, and he was grateful for that. Growing fat this Summer, he'd had a good year so far. There had been stirrings in the animals, rumor that there was more territory for the taking. For so long, animal life had existed at the edge of the two-leggers' world, with only the brave, like the raccoons and the coyotes, daring to venture in to see what these people had to offer. Now, the animals said that the humans were gone. It was safe to cross their big hard paths, and there was no one to chase them away from the nice grass they had in front of their dens. The porcupine didn't know about that... he liked his forest with his berries and his mushrooms.

The night passed with the comings and goings of nocturnal animal life. The bear traveled several miles that night, continuing to forage and fatten himself in preparation for the Winter. He thought back to the nice meal he'd just had. He would have to come back another time to see if there were scraps for him to nibble.

EXTINCTION

It was early in the morning, the sun still barely climbing over the horizon. It created a glow over the trees and jagged skyline. Katy was awake in the soft light of the master bedroom. She sat on the edge of the bed, naked. Katy turned her head to the side and ran her fingers through her hair. The gray that used to be a few sparkling strands now came through in thick bands of white around her temples in her otherwise pitch-black hair. She admired the way it sparkled when it caught the light. Brushing out her hair, she hummed to herself. Jenny sniffed around at her feet and sighed, plopping down on the carpet.

"Dear Jenny, I think it is time for us to take a trip." She bent down and scratched behind the dog's ear. "We'll come back here, of course, though—this is home now." Jenny's tongue lolled out of her mouth, and her eyes shut as she leaned into Katy's hand.

A few hours later, the car was loaded full of supplies for a long trip. Katy drove down the winding driveway and through the forest to downtown Bend. The windows and streets in town looked more scuffed and dirty now. Leaves and dirt littered the streets, and grass sprouted between every crack in the concrete. The more populated an area had once been, the more uncomfortable Katy felt visiting it. She couldn't imagine what these places would look like in ten years, or twenty. Maybe they would be beautiful. For now, they reminded her that she was alone.

"I suppose I might be around to find out, if I don't fall down a damn ridge again," Katy said. She remembered the time her parents had taken her on a hike to a ghost town in Colorado. They'd wanted to show her an example of those small communities abandoned after the Gold Rush or some other situation, which were often high in the mountains or elsewhere inaccessible. The buildings had been faded to a tired gray-brown, showing empty skeletons of homes. Everything had taken on a sleepy, sad hue. Some of the buildings had only been foundations, and others had still had walls and cloudy, mica windows intact. She'd liked carefully walking around the deteriorating buildings, imagining what the people would have been like living there. How long until all of this modern architecture was also a ghost town? Faded to gray and crumbling?

Katy drove for an hour, as she had planned their first stop not far from home. Now that Katy's leg was more or less healed, she had taken to going on long walks through the neighborhood and the forest. Now, it was time for a real hike. As she drove to the trailhead, she massaged her thigh, feeling the dense scar tissue in her leg. The lake was a short drive from town. Jenny paced back and forth in the back of the Subaru, pressing her wet nose to all of the windows and leaving long streaks as they drove down the dirt road. Katy adjusted the rearview mirror so that she could watch Jenny and giggle at the art she left smeared across the passenger windows. Then, it was time to hike. She parked her car neatly at the trailhead, imagining that when she got back down, the lot would be full of other hikers.

The trail wound ever-upward from the start. At first, Katy's steps were slow and wobbly going up the incline, her boots sliding in the loose, dry dirt. Jenny thought she was way too slow and would race up the trail just to come down again like a furry blue and white bullet—only to race back up again as soon as she saw that Katy was, in fact, coming. Sweat trickled down Katy's cheek from her temple. She wiped at and blinked it away. Underneath the pack on her back, her shirt was darkened and wet. Her mind was on the cool bright blue waters of the lake she knew was ahead of her. As she trekked forward, it felt easier and easier to walk, to take big, healthy, normal strides. Looking down, she watched how her leg pumped away underneath her. She knew that, underneath her tough hiking pants, there still was a twisted scar. She really had been incredibly lucky. In fact, she couldn't really think of anyone else who could possibly be as lucky as her at this moment. Katy, seemingly the only person in the whole world to have avoided spontaneously splatting. Who'd then managed to almost die falling down the trail in Yosemite, to only then almost be sucked out of her own bed by whatever had done the splatting of all the humans. Then, to almost die of infection in a hospital bed in a town she didn't even remember the name of. Now she was hiking along with barely a limp in her step as the only damn-lucky person alive. A smile insisted on curling up her lips, and she began to hum as her feet kept a steady beat through the dust.

It took her all day to hike to the summit. She stopped several times to drink water and nibble on deer jerky, and she cupped water in her hands so that Jenny could lap it up happily, though most of it splashed all over Katy's arm instead of going into the dog's mouth. When she came around the corner and saw the mirrored reflection of the lake, her heart jumped in her chest. The water was a bright turquoise greeting the blue sky. The rocky outcrops, the peak of the mountain above, were layered in almost rainbow soil from thousands of years of sediment that had carefully layered themselves into a masterpiece. Dirty old snow still littered shaded areas, as it likely never went away completely even in the middle of Summer. The water was so still that reflections of the clouds above were perfectly printed on the surface. The lake looked like a portal into the sky.

"Ahhhh. Look at that, Jenny. That is what makes life worth living right there. Dont'cha think?" She threw down her pack and pulled off her clothes in a haphazard way, getting tangled in her T-shirt. Jenny got the idea and dove into the water, interrupting the serene quiet of the lake with an exuberant splash.

The small lake was formed from snowy mountain runoff. It was ice cold, and Katy's whole body was covered in goosebumps the second her toes touched the water. The cold made her take short, sharp breaths. Sipping the thin mountain air, she stood for a moment, just wiggling her toes in the ice-cold water. Holding her arms to herself, she waded in, every step sending a jolt through her naked skin. When the water hit her pubic bone, she let out a squeal of discomfort and delight, and then did so again as it hit her ribcage. The cold made her feel wide awake, and also like something was squeezing her chest closed and open at the same time. She took a big breath and sank her head under the water, popping up with a gasp. Jenny came splashing toward her, paws flailing out and scratching Katy's naked skin.

"Nooooo, Jenny!" She laughed and grabbed the swimming dog's body, turning the propeller paws away from her.

A fat marmot was watching them from the rocks above. She seemed indignant that something had disturbed her afternoon slumber and let out a piercing squeak. Katy looked up and laughed at the marmot, who huffed and squeaked again. Her babies all ducked their heads down into the den and hid from the strange visitors below.

Katy and Jenny climbed out of the water together, both shaking off droplets. Katy wrapped herself in a towel she had brought, shivering at the water's edge. The sun was starting to get low in the sky. The high-mountain lake was bathed in a golden sunset light. Her leg cramped and ached, but it was a sweet ache. Massaging it, she watched Jenny lick herself clean and then busy herself with sniffing down the marmot that had been yelling at them earlier.

A while later, once she was dry, Katy made a small fire on the stony earth by the side of the lake and set out sleeping gear. The stars had never looked so bright before, as though they were burning holes in the blanket of the sky. She cooked potatoes she'd found in the cooler of a grocery store that were miraculously still good, mixed with chunks of venison. The ashy smell of the fire tickled her nose as she stirred the food, listening to the hearty sizzle. Her eyes drifted up to the countless other stars that speckled the sky. Maybe some of them, very far away, had life, as well. She pulled the blankets over her and wrapped up in the sleeping bag, thinking about stars and where she was going next. It was time to say goodbye, even though she didn't want to.

It was time to go home to Portland.

The hike down the next morning didn't take her as long as the path up had, but it was still well past noon by the time they made it down to the car again. She ate another simple meal—a can of beans and some meat she had cooked the night before. The fresh venison made her feel so much brighter and healthier than she had over the previous months spent living on only canned food and packages from the stores she'd scavenged. She thought about how nice it would be to have some fresh vegetables, as well. Maybe she should start growing her own food. Yes, soon. She could still plant something simple to harvest before Autumn came. Before that, though, she needed to do something she had been putting off for some time now.

After packing up the car, she drove without stopping. It was only a few hours from Bend to Portland. Katy knew that, if she stopped, she would be tempted to turn around. The roads started to look more familiar, and a nostalgia came over her. She recognized an intersection where she'd used to turn off to go on walks, and then a field where there'd once been some fat old horses, as well as that grocery store where her mom had liked to shop. She passed by her high school and wrinkled her nose at it.

The closer she got to home, the more she tried to pretend she was just coming home for a Summer break, and that her mom and dad would be standing in the driveway when she pulled up. They would laugh and hug her, and then coo over her new dog.

After what felt like too little time, she pulled up into the driveway. As she sat in the car, hands still clutching the steering wheel, she looked at the house where she had grown up. The lawn that her dad had always kept so meticulously green was wispy and dead, and the flowers that lined the entryway were nothing more than finger-like crisps, drooping over the edge of their pots. The winding path up to the front door was barely visible through the dirt and debris. The windows were clouded over, so she couldn't quite see into the living room. Biting her lip, Katy walked the path and stepped onto the faded wood deck. She pulled out her keys and sighed as they fit into the lock and she felt it turn. Jenny waited patiently for the door to open. It swung wide, and Katy hesitated at the entryway.

"Mom, Dad?" It was a hope beyond hope. Her voice echoed through the empty house that smelled of dust and neglect, across the entryway lined with photos of their little family. It was dim without any of the lights on.

"I'm home." She set her backpack down on the bench in the entryway, just as she had always done. She kicked off her hiking boots and walked in. Jenny trotted ahead to explore the house. The kitchen was empty, a single water glass sitting on the counter. It was edged with calc, from water that had long since evaporated. Katy's chest felt tight. She struggled to swallow past the boulder in her mouth, but her tongue was so dry that all she could do was cough a little. She trembled as she looked around the living room, everything still and dark. Her body felt hot, and she shivered at the same time. The green plush couch of her childhood had a book lying on the cushion, a bookmark hanging out about halfway through. Dad's favorite reading spot. She willed herself to walk farther into the house.

Everything in her begged her to turn around and start the car again as she climbed the carpeted stairs that she remembered racing up and down as a child. She rested her hand on the banister that she had carved her name into when she'd been seven, much to the angry disapproval of her mother. She ran her thumb over the clumsy child writing. No, she couldn't delay anymore. She walked into her old bedroom. Mostly, it looked like a storage closet now. Her mom had taken down a lot of her childhood decorations, but Katy's old bed was still the same. Small with pink sheets neatly tucked in, and a big tired-looking stuffed bear sitting on the top. She picked up the bear, hugging it tightly to her chest and ignoring Jenny's eager look at the potential toy. With the bear still tucked under her arm, she turned to walk down the long hallway. At the end was her parents' room. She remembered taking this same walk, the same bear in her arms, as a child when a dream would startle her awake. Just like then, she was trembling with fear, desperate to get to the comfort of family.

Her parents' bedroom had the blinds drawn, dark. It smelled bad, like a year and a half of dust and rot. Trembling, she pulled open the blinds and peered at the bed. Two brown spots peeked at her, just below the pillows.

She stared at those two bloodstains, frozen, squeezing the bear so hard that her biceps trembled.

"Oh, Mom... Daddy." Her voice was small and childlike as her tears started to roll down her face. She crawled onto the bed, curling up around the smelly stains.

"Oh, I'm so sorry." Her cry turned to an ugly sob, hitching and hiccupping in her throat. Her hiccups turned into a wail. The kind of cry that you only heard when someone was truly experiencing the worst heartbreak in life... raw sobs that seem like they never end and are ripped from the very bottom of someone's lungs.

Katy had that kind of cry now, leaving smears of tears on the bed. She ran her hands over the stiff covers, wishing for her parents' touch again. She drowned in a sea of her own tears and snot, barely getting breaths in between howls and sobs.

She cried for what felt like hours. Her forehead felt full, and her eyes puffed up almost to the point of being closed. Her throat ached, and she started using her sleeve as a tissue; it was wet and cold from her snot. She hiccupped as her breathing slowed. *One breath, hic. Two breaths, hic.* Until she fell into a tired mourning sleep, curled up on the edge of the bed.

There was nothing to bury. The next morning, when she woke and cried some more, she went out into the backyard. The wildflowers that her mom had planted at the edge of the property were in full bloom. She remembered when her mom had sprinkled the seeds everywhere, and handed her some to spread, as well. She picked a big bundle of them now, smelling them and squeezing the flowers tightly in her hands. Katy walked across the lawn again and into the dim, musty house. She climbed the stairs one last time and laid the flowers between the two red spots. This house was as good of a casket as any. Tears still stinging her cheeks, she closed their bedroom door behind her. The walk out to the front porch felt like a marathon, every step slow and heavy. She let Jenny trot out the front door as she held it open. The door closed with a finalizing click, and Katy locked it. Still clutching her stuffed bear, she sat on the porch. Her heart ached.

Goodbye. She couldn't bring herself to say her good-byes out loud. The words sounded too open and empty against the big house, with no one to hear them anymore. Even though she didn't believe in that sort of thing, she hoped that there was a good place her parents had gone to after they'd left this world. Somewhere that had wildflowers in the back garden; somewhere that she could see them again someday. The idea was a lot more comforting than the blackness, a more final end that Katy thought likely came to all things.

She sat in the car, staring at the empty house. The neat blue trim, the leaves that were piled up in the front yard. She began to feel tears threatening to spill over her eyelids again and started the car. Driving away, she resisted the urge to look back in the rearview mirror.

She would never come back.

DRIVE

Katy didn't want to go back to Bend yet. No, sitting inside and staring at the walls would mean she would be left alone with her pain and nothing else. For now, they needed to keep moving. The west of the U.S. was a great place to wander, with expansive roads that went on forever—fields and fields wide open. Keeping her focus on the road ahead of the steering wheel, she would turn on a whim, not paying much attention to where she was going. In passing, she thought that she should probably keep track so she wouldn't get endlessly lost. The thought came and went. The first night of travel, she pulled into a gas station and slept in the parking lot after folding down the seats of the car. Jenny slept curled up with her, keeping her warm. In the morning, she sat out on the asphalt, cooking breakfast, watching the sun rise red and angry over the mountains in the distance.

"I'm going to Colorado," she said to herself, recognizing the road. She munched on crackers and jerky, letting the crumbs fall all down her front and to the ground.

"I miss eggs," she mused. Jenny didn't seem to miss eggs, and loudly chewed on her piece of jerky, making smacking sounds as she moved the piece of meat to the back of her jaws in order to get a better purchase on the tough food.

Before leaving the gas station, Katy went to the door of the convenience store. Normally, she would just pry the doors to buildings open so that she could neatly close them behind her. She started to put the crowbar in its place now, though, and then hesitated. Raising the bar high over her head, she swung it hard into the glass door. It stuck through the glass the first time as the glass around it crumpled. It didn't shatter like she'd expected. Yanking the crowbar loose, she swung again. This time, there was a satisfying crash as the glass shattered to the ground. She knocked the rest of the glass out of the frame with big sweeping blasts. Once she was through, she proceeded to do the same to all of the windows. Once she was inside, her foot lashed out and kicked over a stand of chips. Another swing of the crowbar brought the cash registers flying off of the counter and into the beer cooler. Picking up a heavy car battery charger, Katy flung it into the soda cooler window. It bounced off and left a spiderweb of cracks. Jenny seemed to know when Katy was in one of her moods and had stayed outside, basking in the sun on the asphalt.

Satisfied with her mayhem, Katy gathered items off the shelves that remained. Most of the food in a gas station had so many preservatives in it that there wasn't much rotten-smelling there. Beef jerky to bolster her supplies of venison, hostess cakes, peanuts. When food was scarce, it didn't matter so much what was "healthy" or not. The calories were good, the sugar was gold, and any time there was an opportunity to eat with some variety, she took it. She hefted cases of water out of their resting places in the back room and scooted them into a neat pile near the door—to be loaded into the car. She hesitated when walking past the coolers and decided on a six-pack of beer that she placed neatly on top of the mountain of water. On the way out of the now shattered door, she took a pair of sunglasses from the rack and put them on. She felt like a badass in an action movie, with the tag still dangling on the side. Jenny was sitting in the back of the car when she came out, avoiding Katy's gas station violence. Her tail wagged in a greeting that became even more wide and sweeping when Katy produced a handful of dog treats from her pocket. Gas stations were strange places. They had snacks for the road, sometimes souvenirs, and usually a small practical goods section where dog food, condoms, and cleaning supplies were always grouped together in a questionable order.

Still thinking about eggs, Katy went on the road again. *I wonder if I could find some chickens and catch them.* The idea of runny golden yolks and bacon made her mouth water. She had seen cattle that had been free-range running around, and maybe some chickens had survived if they hadn't been locked up in some coop when their owners had gone poof. If she could just catch a few, she could build a coop back at the house. The cows were something she had considered, as well. One step at a time, though. Everything was a lot more work when you were only one person, and she didn't plan on getting gored by a horn or kicked by a cow in a way that would result in a slow, painful death.

Katy took to driving again. The hours went on, and she took few breaks. When she did take them, she would let Jenny out of the car and explore the town they were passing through. Every place was the same. Dusty, abandoned buildings without a hint of human life. The wild reclaiming it on the edges. She would take out her can of spray paint and write the same thing on the town sign or, extra-large, on the road itself.

ALIVE IN BEND - 681 Ponderosa Dr

Maybe someday, someone else would be there to read them. Katy wondered if the sign would still be true then. Would she still be alive in Bend in a few years? Did she want to be? She wiped her hands on her pants where the spray paint had leaked onto her fingertips. She squinted into the hot morning sun.

Did she want to be?

EVERYTHING BURNS

One evening, after passing the state border into Utah, Katy was watching the sun set. She left her car parked across both lanes of the old dried-out highway. The world was theirs. Standing in the middle of the road, she threw a ball for Jenny off into the scrub brush and desert sand. The tennis ball would come back to her sticky and wet, with dirt and sticks clinging to its spongy outside. Katy would give it a shake, in a useless attempt to get rid of some of the muck, and wind up to throw it again. Jenny would shoot off like a furry bullet out of a gun, her rear end close to the dirt, kicking up the red dust as she sped after the prized ball. She was a very fast dog. At a similar pace on the way back to Katy, she would look at Katy gleefully, tongue hanging out one side of her mouth with the ball tucked into her other cheek.

The wind-up and swing of the ball put a healthy burn into Katy's arm, and she watched the dog shoot off into the overgrown hay grass yet again. The high desert plain was quite beautiful, edged with the mountains in the distance. The sun was about to slip behind the jagged skyline, and it was cold. Up here, it didn't matter what time of the year it was; the air always had a bite to it. Jenny jumped in the air and barked to get Katy's attention back to the very important task of throwing the ball. She leaned against the car after throwing the ball again, enjoying the warmth still radiating off of the engine. Her cheeks were red and chafed from the wind.

Katy waved her hand at Jenny, who sat panting expectantly at her feet. "In a minute."

Katy looked out across the red-brown landscape, exploring the sensation of the cool wind biting at her skin. She watched the sage and juniper wave in the breeze that would die down as the sun set further. An alien landscape with no life except for them in sight. She looked toward the crown of red-rock and saw a strange smudge of clouds across the horizon.

"Strange," Katy mused, opening up the back of the car and rustling around for everything they needed to stay there for the night.

A short while later, she was sitting on a pillow next to the right rear tire of the car, poking gently at the fire she had so carefully willed into existence in the middle of the road. She had found enough scrub brush and a dead juniper tree to make a modest fire to warm herself by. Jenny was curled up right next to her, back pressed against Katy's thigh. Katy picked up a thin branch from the pile of tinder next to her and dangled it into the fire, watching the tip smoke and burst into a small golden flame.

The sun had slipped past the horizon and the last of its glow was leaving the sandy landscape. Katy watched her smudge of smoke wind upward in a dancing pattern and disappear into the sky as the stars flickered into existence in the clear night. Before full darkness came, the sky was a teal blue. Since she had started driving away from Portland, she had avoided thinking about her parents. Now, she looked into that expansive sky and thought about them. She remembered all of the good times of her childhood, and the bad. She remembered their smiles and the way that they'd laughed. She remembered how kind her father had been, and how wicked her mother's tongue could be at the wrong moment. No tears threatened to fall. She was only honoring their memories.

"I remember you," she said to the sky as another star became visible.

"I don't want to be here without you. But I remember." Her voice cracked, and she squeezed Jenny's soft fur.

A wave of despair washed over her, giving her goosebumps. Then, a sense of peace. This roller coaster was inside of her most of the time. It was always a battle to stay on top of the hill instead of plummeting downward.

"Oh, what do I do? What do I do?" Now, she let herself cry a little.

Once the fire had died down, she crawled into the back of the car, moving into her nest of blankets. Jenny hopped up and took her typical spot at her feet. She fell asleep quickly, into a deep and dreamless sleep.

The next morning, she packed up quickly and efficiently, squinting toward the horizon where she had seen something odd in the air. Still, there was an ominous gray smudge across the skyline.

"Let's go see what that's about." Katy tossed the last supplies into the back and closed it up.

About forty minutes later, she passed the friendly green sign that said, "Salt Lake City 15 miles." As she wound down the mountain pass, she saw smoke rising from where she knew the city to be below. Not a small campfire smoke, but angry smudges across the sky. As she got closer, she could see that the whole sky glowed an angry gray and red.

"Shit." As the city bloomed into view, she saw that it was a black crater of what it had once been. The air was still heavy with smoke and ash that snowed down on her windshield like a Winter storm. On the high ground, before the highway dipped down into the valley where Salt Lake sat, she had a view of it all. The tall buildings were crumbled skeletons of what they'd once been. It was as though one section of the world had turned to black and white. The wind buffeted her as she got out of the car—the air was still sickly hot, with the acrid smell of a fire of glass and plastic and gasoline. Katy coughed and pulled her T-shirt over her mouth, keeping Jenny closed up in the car. Her eyes watered as the poison in the air stung them, and she struggled to take in the destruction in front of her. She could only stand being outside for a few moments and got back into the car to look from there. The heat from the fire, even as it died out, was painful.

The fire had wiped out the majority of the city. Katy drove as close as she dared, staying on the highway. Her tire treads left deep imprints through the ash. The heat was even worse here, and she could see areas where the fire still smoldered. One of the taller buildings downtown was but a skeleton of charred metal, and leaning dangerously on its neighbor.

So many events could have started a fire like this. Electrical failure; a stove left on. She was amazed to see what had happened, with a fire left unchecked in the middle of an abandoned city. The buildings that weren't burned to the ground had ashy windows. The fire must have happened some time ago, but still, every time the wind picked up, ashes danced through the air and pockets of flame smoldered beneath the protected surface of ash and rubble. Jenny was standing on the armrest of the passenger seat, staring out the window with her nose pressed to the glass. An eerie silence blanketed the charred city.

"Wow." She looked up at one glass building, a skeleton standing thirteen stories high. The wind picked up again, and she heard a tired, creaking sound.

The fire must have burned for weeks. She drove at a snail's pace on the highway, ogling the destruction around her. The many towns and cities she had been in since people had left had been pristine, only showing the signs of nature quietly retaking what had always been hers. Time hadn't had a chance to chew away at human architecture much yet. Salt Lake City was different, though; Salt Lake City was a graveyard of human development.

Salt Lake City was a funeral pyre.

Katy shivered and wrapped the scarf she was wearing around her face, pressing down on the gas to drive away. She felt like a mouse walking through the charred remains of some unknown giants who were staring down at her, threatening to collapse at any moment. Or even worse, grow back their flesh and chase her. For some distance, she still didn't dare get out of the car, as the air was thick and ashy even miles away from the center of the fire. Her bladder complained about the lack of a break, but she pushed on. She would stop once the air didn't look like a smoker's lung. The charred city shrank in her rearview mirror, and she watched the whole time it did, happy to see it go.

Katy thought about wildfires as she drove away from Salt Lake City. The kind that raged through a dry Summer forest, consuming everything in their path. The kind that humans had desperately tried to control for years, to avoid such hungry fires consuming expensive houses. In college, she had learned about the real nature of forest fires, and that they had raged through forests long before people had been around to put them out. She knew how it worked: Forests have trees that die, undergrowth that is dry and old. Then, one Summer, there is a tiny spark in the air and it burns through everything. The dead trees, old grass… everything that was built up in the forest is burned clean. Through the ashes, a new forest can grow with the fertile earth that is left behind. Animals begin coming back to the edges of the charred forest, and it comes back healthier. Trees like pines rely on these fires for their reproduction, the pinecones opening up and planting their seeds in the ashy earth.

Humans had unwittingly avoided letting the smaller fires burn, and let this build-up happen for too long. Now, the earth had wildfires that consumed more and more. She guessed a big one would rage through some of the forests of the western U.S. in the next few years, with no one to try to stop it. The thought made her shudder. The regrowth would come back stronger, and without the meddling of humans. A new forest without bounds of houses and human development.

Salt Lake City had had a wildfire burn, but the buildings didn't leave behind hungry seeds to soak up the nutrients of the burn-off. No new skyscrapers would take their places. Maybe, after some time, some plants would find their way back to the concrete and steel world. Maybe Salt Lake City would be one of the first places that nature would reclaim the humans' territory. Katy made a note to come back in a few years if she was still alive so that she could see it again.

Perhaps a forest would sprout out of the ashes, and it would be beautiful.

REGROWTH

Several hundred miles later, Katy had looped back northward.

After a short breakfast, Katy and Jenny were ready to head into Boise. She had done a marathon of driving to get away from Salt Lake. The whole time, she'd kept looking in her rearview mirror to watch as the smoke that streaked across the sky had begun to disappear into the distance. The red-dust desert landscape of Utah had given way to the flat tan fields of Idaho. A year of no farming meant that the neat squares of farmland were empty squares of dirt and shriveled harvests from last year.

Katy had never been to Boise before. She didn't think she'd been missing much, as she drove past what she considered a terribly bland landscape. Jenny began to grow restless in the back, scrambling back and forth over her gear and whining.

"Okay, okay. We'll find a place to take a break for a while." Katy turned off the main highway.

Katy could tell this was farming country as she drove past houses with tractors parked in front and more farming supply stores than she'd known existed in the whole world. And then, a smell worse than any smell she had ever encountered before suddenly assaulted her through the air conditioning system.

"Oh, what the *hell* is that?" Katy clasped her hand over her nose and gagged. She found out soon enough. It was a stock field, where cattle had been herded in huge numbers before going to slaughter. The flies were a black cloud that she could see from a distance, and the crows and buzzards another black cloud on top of that one.

The cattle at stock fields typically stood in their own shit and mud for weeks, their noses buried in the asses of their neighbors. Wet, scared, and without enough space to move. Even when the cows had been alive, these places had stunk. The smell of a cattle processing area could make a whole city smell of cow shit when the wind blew the wrong direction. Despite her common-sense urge to keep driving, Katy pulled to the side to look closer. The road was relatively close to the pen, which must have been awful when all of the cows had still been alive. A few more car lengths on the soft muddy side of the road, and she was right up next to the pen.

About three hundred dead cows were piled on top of each other in the tiny paddock. It had been some time since they had died. The smell was worse than anything she had ever smelled before, and she imagined it was what a battlefield would smell like, the rot of that many bodies. Her hands were clasped to her mouth in horror. Empty eye sockets gazed sightlessly up at the blue sky, the animals' mouths open in dying gapes. The few that hadn't been picked of all of their internal organs had hides that were drawn tight over their bodies, jagged-looking bones poking through the shriveled fur. All of these cows had starved to death and died on top of each other, to become food for the very fat-looking crows and vultures. Even with the windows rolled up, the smell was making Katy's eyes water and her stomach churn. When she felt her mouth start to water with that tell-tale vomit feeling, she turned the car away so fast that her tires spewed dirt as she climbed back to the road. Even as her eyes went back to the road and she sped away, though, she still saw the cattle piled there. The one with its rib cage opened wide to the sky, ribbons of fur and flesh hanging off of the stained bones reaching out, as if to cry for help. The birds tearing into the bursting bodies. She guessed that image would never leave her. The skeleton of Salt Lake and the skeletons of those forgotten in the stock fields.

It was only about five hours more of driving between Boise and Bend. Katy arrived long before the sun was going to set. She wound up the familiar driveway as Jenny squealed her delight and wagged her tail furiously.

"Jenny, come on!" Katy called from the door. She was eager to get inside. Something about being home always felt so good. No matter if you were gone for a few hours or for a few weeks like she had been.

Jenny finally came after sniffing around the yard some more. Katy kicked off her shoes at the entrance and walked through the halls barefoot. Hers. Home had never felt so good. Her bare feet pattered on the hardwood and tile floors as she traced the walls with her fingertips. Her home. Even in all of this madness, she had a place to call her own. One where she had weathered out the worst mental storms. Now, she came home with an added peace of mind. She had done the one thing she had put off for so long.

She opened a warm beer and walked to the back windows. In the almost dark, she could see a black bear sniffing around the fire. He had come back a few times, hoping there would be some more fresh venison sitting out for him.

A few hours later, Katy stretched out on the king-sized bed and sighed. Being in a soft bed after so many nights spent curled up in the back of the car felt great. The knots in her muscles felt like they were melting away in the plush bedding. The sheets on her naked body, cool to the touch in the warm night, sent a tingle to just below her belly button. Katy had been single for a long time before the world had ended for humans, but now the lack of human touch made her ache. She wished for a mate, as she assumed most animals did. Especially when she was ovulating, there were nights where she almost couldn't sleep thinking about that need, that want that was always there. She had never planned on having children—the idea hadn't interested her much. Now, there was nothing more that she wanted than to have a full, fat belly with another human in it. A human who could keep her company, who she could raise and care for. She held her stomach with one hand and fell asleep caressing her empty womb.

BEAR COMPANY

"Hey!" Katy shouted from the back deck, naked.

She waved her arms back and forth. "Get out of there!"

The bear lifted his head from the compost tub Katy had made at the end of the yard. He'd had his face buried into the old leaves and food waste, munching away. Inside the house, Jenny was barking wildly and even clawing at the glass of the back door.

The human and the dog yelling at him didn't seem to concern the huge brown-furred bear. He finished munching the bone he had found and turned away just as Katy finished gathering rocks to throw at him. Katy watched his round rump disappear into the forest and sighed as she turned to go back inside.

The days had turned into weeks, the weeks into months. Katy had fallen into a routine. Wake up, continue her attempts at her first year of gardening, spend the afternoon napping or throwing the ball for Jenny. *Rinse and repeat.* Peppered into her attempted farming routine, she would take drives to nearby towns to ransack art supplies or books. Gardening had a steeper learning curve than she'd expected. She had started too late, on top of that, and many of her little plants had barely sprouted. Then there was the issue of water. With no hose to pull over to the garden beds, Katy hadn't yet figured out a solution that would give her a ready stream of water. She was getting closer to a plan, though, after days of staring at different irrigation books that were currently spread across the dining room table.

Despite her late efforts, Katy knew that it would likely be next year before she was able to sustain herself on her own land. Luckily, food wasn't scarce. It might be the end of the world for humanity, but at least Katy wasn't competing with other humans for resources. Often, that thought kept Katy entertained for hours. All of the movies and books she had read about the apocalypse had been about people. How people would act, how they would band together and become barbarians fighting each other. She'd never liked those books and movies much.

Katy put on a pair of work pants and a sports bra. Her skin was the darkest it had ever been from so much time spent in the sun. She opened the sliding glass door, and Jenny bolted outside to do her usual rounds around the house. Jenny never went far from Katy, most of the time content to be her shadow. Every morning, she would take a break from Katy to disappear into the woods. She would be back sometime around midday, though, panting heavily and ready to rest in the shade as Katy spent her day around the house.

Today wasn't any different. Katy worked in the morning to clear away pine needles and broken sticks from an area she planned to plant, and Jenny came back around lunchtime to remind her to eat. She ruffled the dog's thick soft fur and went inside.

After slurping down some pasta cooked over her camp stove, Katy flopped onto the plush leather sofa. Before she knew it, her eyes fell closed and she slipped into a dream.

The world was blanketed in thick white snow. No longer was the hot late-Summer sun warming the backyard. It was cold, and the wind was howling against the big glass windows of the house. Katy got up from the couch and stretched her arms.

"Come to the forest."

Katy jumped and looked around for the voice. The voice was deep and rumbling like an earthquake. For a moment, Katy looked wildly around for any sign of the pitch-black smoke that had haunted her. Nothing was there. Jenny was sleeping peacefully by the lit fireplace, her head resting on her front paws.

Katy stood, drawn to the back door. She slid it open and let the burst of freezing cold air hit her body. She wrapped a blanket around her shoulders and shivered. Jenny didn't wake up, her chest rising and falling in a deep sleep. Katy's bare feet stung against the cold snow as she stepped out onto the deck. The snow was deep enough that her feet disappeared up to the ankles as she trudged across the deck and down the stairs. Ahead of her, she could see the tree line, obscured with a mist of snow kicked up by the wind. It was night, but the white sky from the blizzard kept it light enough to see.

Deeper into the forest she went. Past the area where she would explore for mushrooms in the Spring and Summer. Past one of her usual loops she would take with Jenny when they went on a stroll. She climbed over slick rocks and outcroppings.

Movement in the trees ahead of her caught her eyes, and she crouched down to avoid being seen. Massive antlers untangled from the branching pine trees. A buck was walking toward her. A dark silhouette, slowly coming one step after the other toward where Katy was trying to hide. She thought she could see something glimmer in the center of its forehead.

The three-eyed buck stopped, staring at her.

SELKIE

The cold ocean spray hit her face. Her skin stung in every spot where the rough, misted waters touched her skin. Sea bees. She stood at the jagged shoreline, watching the waves foam and stir against the rocks. The west coast of the U.S. was a pensive place in the Autumn and Winter months. Gray and dark, with sweeping winds near the ocean. Listening to the waves and feeling the salt of the water had always cleared Katy's mind and provided some comfort from whatever might be bothering her. Coming here had become a habit. Every few weeks, she would feel the urge and drive hours to make the trip. She knew that she wouldn't always be able to do so. At some point, gasoline would degrade and there would be no more driving. Then her movement would be much more limited. The freedom was part of what kept her going at this point, and she dreaded the day that it would go away. As Winter had crept across the landscape again, Katy had lost her daily routine that kept her busy and distracted.

Dreams had begun to haunt her again. She was restless.

She stood on the jagged coastline, looking down at the turbulent ocean. The waves would burst against the rocks below in a cascade of white, angry water that contrasted with the dark gray sky. It looked dangerous. Katy knew the safe places to climb down and take a dip, away from the crashing waves and rip currents. Her face was wet from the spray of the Winter ocean.

Despite the cold and the damp, she made her way down through the rocks. Placing each hand carefully among the rough outcrops, stepping down onto the small spit of a beach. The sky was dark, with a storm rolling in. Coal black clouds pregnant with punishing cold rains were approaching on the skyline. Jenny stood above her, pacing back and forth, starting to lean forward to jump down and then hesitating and pacing again. The dog normally liked water, but the last time they had been there, an abnormally large wave had smashed her against the rocks. Since then, Jenny had contented herself with whining from the rocks above until Katy was done with her Winter swim.

Katy stood facing the waves, her hands shoved deep into her thick jacket with the hood pulled up high. The storm wouldn't be coming for real for some time. The sand whipped up from the beach, spraying her pants in a patter. A seal was lying on the beach a ways away from her, staring in her direction with its deep puppy-like eyes. It seemed unconcerned with her and the dog, and only continued to bob its head up and down, flippers resting on the wet sand. Katy thought about the myth of the selkies she had learned about as a child. Selkies were women who were also seals, who could shed their pelts and walk as humans, and then wrap their warm pelt around themselves again and escape to the sea. How she wished she could slip into a fur and become a seal. Join the seal going off into the ocean to eat good fish; lie with the other seals. To be with others of her kind, instead of being the last one. A seal would be a much more useful shape than this human one, cast aside from the technology and the cars. Without the things they built, humans were nothing. The least adapted to the harsh environments around them. The wish left a deep longing in Katy that had been building as time passed by. She never truly had adjusted to her solitude. She didn't think that was actually possible. Oh, to be with others.

She unzipped her heavy jacket with steady hands and dropped it to the ground behind her. She pulled off her sweater and her pants. Standing naked on the shore, she closed her eyes and began to wade into the ice-cold water. The seal harrumphed in agreement and inched into the waves. The shock of the cold made Katy's heart beat faster as she dove into the water head-first after the first few icy footsteps. She came up for air with a gasp and looked back at the coastline. Her hands squeezed open and closed, feeling the cold water running between her tingling fingers. She breathed in the air, salty water stinging her eyes as she blinked them open and closed again. Jenny was barking at her, wagging her tail and trying to jump down to the beach again. She didn't see the seal anymore. It had probably slid into secret depths where she could not follow, to dream deep ocean dreams and fly through the water.

After the initial stabbing cold, a warmth traveled through her body as she treaded water. She licked the sea salt off of her lips and turned around toward the shore. She had half a mind to turn around and swim out into the ocean, as far as she could go. Until there was nothing around her but the rolling waves, the dark below. To be surrounded by the cold expanse of the ocean as the storm rolled in, bringing more wet from above. The idea thrilled her and made her heart beat even faster. *No, it's not time yet*, a voice in her head told her, with some certainty. *Not time... yet.* Her feet slipped on some rocks and kelp tangled her feet. *There is still something to do here. I'm not sure what, though.* She found purchase on the rocks and climbed out of the water to her warm, welcoming clothes. A short Winter swim.

Steam came off of her scarred body as she climbed out of the water. She imagined that she looked ethereal, like she was glowing. Though she didn't know it, she very well could have been a selkie pulling off her pelt, if anyone had been there to watch her. With the coat wrapped around her and shivering with her breath gathering out of her nostrils in puffs of smoke, she climbed back up the rocks. With newly wet and cold hands, she felt the rough rock bite into her hands more than it had on her descent. She was greeted at the top by a wriggling, warm dog who licked her face eagerly, tasting the ocean, and in some ways scolding her for running away where

Jenny couldn't follow. Jenny crawled over Katy's lap, and Katy kept staring out to the ocean, thinking about the foaming waves and the seal that was likely below them. Still, her heart wanted to follow those dark flippers into the ocean.

Katy sat there shivering, losing herself in deep thought. Everything here was a cycle. Energy didn't disappear or reappear from nothing, and every single action made for an equal and opposite reaction. The tide came in, and it went out again, pulled by the gravitational force of the moon. When an animal died, its organic matter was recycled, eaten by small scavengers. The small scavengers were then eaten by a bigger animal, that could then give birth to more offspring because it was well-fed. The energy was never actually destroyed.

Katy stroked Jenny's fur with her clammy hands, the long hairs sticking to her fingers. At first, Katy hadn't understood how every person could disappear with almost no trace and have no other effects on the world. Now, she understood, as she watched a lone piece of plastic float across the water and then crash repeatedly into the rocks below her.

Humans had begun down a path of energy consumption, building up their byproducts in this world. Scientists had known that something was going to happen, that the world was changing because of humanity's presence. They'd always thought, *Someday, someday, but not now.* But plastics had filled the oceans to create giant islands that no one lived on. The glaciers slowly melted away, inching back from their original resting places. Animals disappeared for humanity's benefit, sport, or simply because of negligence. And there'd been no price paid. The bill had come due, however, and this was the equal and opposite reaction. Humans were no more. Though Katy couldn't explain the exact details of this with her scientific knowledge, the fate of humanity was clear to her.

At least, that was how Katy saw it. If another person had been left behind, say a Christian, they would have been speaking of the rapture. Maybe it was all the same, but she just had different words for it.

Katy drove back home. She left her wet clothes by the door and stepped into a warm, fluffy robe. The big house was welcoming, familiar. During her travels, she'd picked up things she liked. She walked through the house to keep herself warm before crouching in front of the living room fireplace to light a fire. Her eyes wandered across the living room as she stoked the small fire. A painting from a gallery that she would never have been able to afford in her regular life was hung over the big fireplace, and there was a sculpture of a deer jumping nearby. The antlers from the buck she had killed a few Summers ago were resting on the mantle. She had bleached them a bright white and admired them on cold evenings as she sat curled up in a pile of blankets on the couches. Jenny was sitting in front of the cold fireplace expectantly. She had grown into a fluffy, wide-backed dog, from the skinny puppy that Katy had picked up. Her ears stood up now, except for a tiny lip at the top that still flopped over. Katy stacked logs into the fireplace from the pile next to it. Jenny rested her head on her paws and watched Katy work with her bright blue eyes.

Once the fire was roaring and the grate placed back on, Katy boiled some water with the camp stove she had set up on top of the fancy range in the kitchen. She made herself some tea and sat in front of the fire, petting Jenny, who sighed and rested her head on Katy's lap. Katy powered up the cell phone, which she mostly left off these days. The date was December 18th. Her birthday had been a few weeks ago, whatever that meant. It hadn't been her real birthday anyway, since she'd been adopted and didn't know the actual day of her birth. When *it* had happened, she had been twenty-seven, and now she was thirty-one years old.

The years had gone by quickly, with her routine and her home. Time didn't pass in the same way anymore, and there had been periods of months where she had completely lost track. The only thing that ruled her time-keeping was the change of the seasons. When she felt the first crispness of Autumn (often before that, as well), she would get busy preparing for Winter. The Spring was for one of her walkabout trips, where she would explore a new wilderness area and the cities around it. Summer was for lazy days, writing, and some hunting if she didn't have enough food.

The two of them sat there in their comfortable silence, watching the logs spit and crackle.

DEER SONG

Air flew into her lungs as she gasped awake, clutching handfuls of her sheets. Her body was outlined in sweat. She looked around the room and saw nothing out of the ordinary. Jenny was next to the bed, sound asleep. She didn't stir with Katy's thrashing.

Come into the forest.

The voice echoed through her head. She rubbed her temples; her mind felt like it was swimming. Every movement came through glue, slow and heavy.

Come to me.

She must be hallucinating again. She had been doing so well. She hadn't gone on a rampage of paint in so long, or drunk herself into a stupor. Something willed her out of the bed. She let the feeling tug her. What did she have to lose? It had been so long since something had called to her like this, she wanted to answer. She pulled on clothes with sleep-fumbling hands. Jenny still didn't awaken. She went and shook the dog. Still, she did not wake up. Katy checked to see if she was breathing. She was, but in a deep, almost bewitched sleep. This dream had come many times now and was always the same. Still, she would always try to wake Jenny.

Please come.

There was some urgency in that tickle in her mind. She sat at the entrance of the house and pulled on her boots. She left the door behind her wide open, in case the dog wanted to follow later. The air was cold... it was probably the early hours of the morning at this point, but she hadn't checked. She started walking into the deeper part of the forest, away from town. She let that tickle in the back of her head guide her, giving in to the urgent need it gave her.

Something else was in the forest. She stopped, the snow crunching beneath her boots. There was a light dusting of it on everything, making everything shimmer in the early light. Through the rare mountain-mists of early morning, something was walking toward her. Unlike her footsteps that sent a whole percussion of cracks and crunches, it was silent as it walked. Katy stepped farther into the clearing and waited. Her black and shock-white hair fell into her face, but she didn't brush it out of the way.

A brilliant white deer walked forward, glowing silver antlers radiating through the wispy air. His steps were even, measured. Every movement was careful and knowing. They stood facing each other. He regarded her carefully, looking at the way she stood and her sinewy frame. His eyes were not liquid brown deer eyes, with the square-shaped pupils she expected. They looked more like her eyes, full of intelligence and rounded pupils.

"You led me here, didn't you?" Katy asked. Her breath produced puffs of smoke in the cold air.

His massive head tilted down. *Yes.*

"Are you going to make me a red spot?" she asked. She knew the answer was no. She also knew he had the answers she had spent her entire life seeking and not finding. She told herself to be patient, that the world didn't move as fast now and neither did she.

His nose tilted slightly to the left. *No?* Katy guessed. The air puffed out of his velvety nostrils in thick clouds. Their breath hung in clouds in the space between them, mingling before spreading out to invisible.

Jenny trotted up beside Katy, much to her surprise. In her dreams, Jenny never came. Katy prepared to yell at Jenny not to chase the stag, but she did not. The dog sat down at Katy's heel and watched the stag, almost thoughtfully.

"Do you know what happened to everyone?" She crossed her arms against the cold. Katy realized that she could feel the cold biting into her skin. She had never felt that before in her dreams. Was this real?

"Why was I left behind?" she asked, and let a few tears fall down her cheek. The streak they left was a cold sting on her face.

"Was I an accident? But why didn't you take me away like you did the woman in the white room? Was she an accident, too?" Her words started to bubble up despite herself.

The deer said nothing, but folded his long legs beneath him, sitting down carefully. Katy continued to stand. The deer did not speak. Despite his glittering third eye, unblinking, he was just a deer. Katy thought the answer was yes. *Yes*, she was an accident. *Yes*, this world had swallowed up the woman from the white room.

"So, you left me here to watch this world without us?" She sat down, too, not caring that the snow was soaking through her pants. The bubble of anger she had for a moment floated away as she sat close to the beast. "What are you?"

His nose touched her leg, and a ripple of energy flowed through her.

"We were hurting you, weren't we?" She gently placed her hand on his nose, letting the wild energy flow through her. She could feel it rattle her teeth, and every hair on her body was standing on end. "We were tearing this world apart, and finally you needed to shake us off like an itch."

The deer said nothing. The third eye in the middle of his forehead was the only one that remained open, gazing forward sightlessly as he calmly closed his other two eyes.

She crumpled to the ground, letting out a wet sob. Her hands flopped to her sides, palms up. The loneliness came over her in waves, with the years of wandering the mountains and swimming in the coldest lakes. The days spent manic, talking to herself and painting more and darker, twisted paintings. Katy mourned it all in that moment. The pain, the enduring pain. No matter how many landscapes she walked across, or how many books she read, that loneliness was always there. Her sobs echoed across the trees and wide valleys.

A warm nose touched the top of her head, reducing her to sniffles instead of the wide sobs that had been disturbing the quiet early-morning forest.

Katy looked into his eyes, seeing all three of them open. *Would I like to stay?* Katy thought to herself. She wondered if the thought truly was her own, or if the deer was speaking to her in his own way. *Would she like to stay?*

Katy paused. All of those years of suffering, alone. Although she had been desperate for human contact, it was so beautiful here. She had seen so much more of the world than she would have if she had been locked to human responsibilities. The companions she had met along the way—Old Dog, Jenny. They had given her years of laughter and unconditional love. Would she want to stay? Until she was old and wrinkled? A long wait for the sweet escape of death, where she could finish more paintings. The decision was a hard one, harder than she might have expected. Maybe a few years ago, she would have answered no immediately and begged to be taken from this place.

"Yes. Yes, I'd like to stay." She looked up at his glowing antlers.

"But... I'm so lonely. I don't want to stay like... this." She gestured to herself. "I just want some company... please."

"More than anything." She stood up again, wiping her wet hands on her pants. Her heart was racing with fear and excitement. She knew this was the end of something. Not her life, but something. Endings usually hurt, goodbyes even worse, but this time she only felt excited. Now, it was finally time. She was ready.

The deer's third eye looked right at her, through her. Katy looked down at Jenny one more time. She was sitting at her heel, beautiful plush fur ruffling in the light breeze that had picked up through the trees. Jenny looked back at her, eyes full of love. It was time to come home.

He jumped forward, his antler piercing Katy's chest. The antler dove between her ribs and deep into her heart. Katy gasped and gripped the sides of the bone that had stabbed into her. She looked down. Katy didn't feel pain. Instead, a tingling started and burst through her whole body. She screamed—the last human scream. Her hands gripped the velvety antler, slipping on her own blood. She could hear Jenny's barking, but it was distant, down the long hallway of the end.

Her head drooped, and the deer tilted his head. Her body tilted with it, but she still didn't feel any pain. Impaled on the sharp antlers, the tingling feeling in her body grew. Her eyes lulled closed, and she imagined the warmth of a fireplace, the patterns behind her eyelids dancing as the wood crackled and the light danced. The ache of the cold air disappeared from her limbs. Her body started to shift, bones growing larger and changing shape. It didn't hurt, though; she just observed the feeling with interest, suspended in the air. Then, she let go. Let go of all of the pain, the suffering of her life. She let go of all the good things, too. The dogs who had kept her company, her childhood. It all slipped away. She let her eyes close.

She let go into the darkness.

A MOTHER'S PEACE

Autumn, the time of sleep. A ripe time, where the world lets go. To begin anew, but not quite yet. The time for rains that will wet the ground for a new year, the end of a cycle. The dying but also the birth of the new. The birds move to their Winter homes in a time of leaving. Mammals grow their heavy Winter coats and fatten themselves up with the sweets of Summer. The trees change to colors of rich golds, yellows, and reds.

The bear crawled into the hole she would slumber in for the next three months, her home in a dark, cold place. Her rich brown fur ruffled in the cold air, and her wet black nose wiggled in the fall smells. The world was still hurting, but it was healing, as well. All of the trees drew inward, taking their colors away for a period of quiet, but there would be rebirth after this. She turned around in circles, getting comfortable on the cool earth in her den. She pulled the dirt and snow to cover the entrance, staring up at the blue sky one last time. The air blew its goodbye kiss to her, and the hormones telling her to sleep throbbed in her fat body. The hormones made her sleepy and slower. She had found a good den this year, as the other bears had stayed well away from her territory. They didn't like her much; even as solitary creatures, most of them avoided her with wide berths. Something about her smell… she was different. She had an old smell, a smell many of the bears knew from a time before and from a creature that no longer walked the forests. During the Summers and Springs, this bear also walked through the forests with a dog. Now, the dog would spend the Winter on her own. But they would be together again when the bear awoke.

The sleep began to come over her. The long sleep, the longest next to death. She rested her head on her massive paws, letting her breath slow and become shallow. Her stomach was full with the fruits of the Summer, and also with something else. New life was blooming inside of her—one that would greet the new Spring with her. She was pregnant.

She wouldn't be alone anymore.

CPSIA information can be obtained
at www.ICGtesting.com
Printed in the USA
FSHW011726150421
80519FS